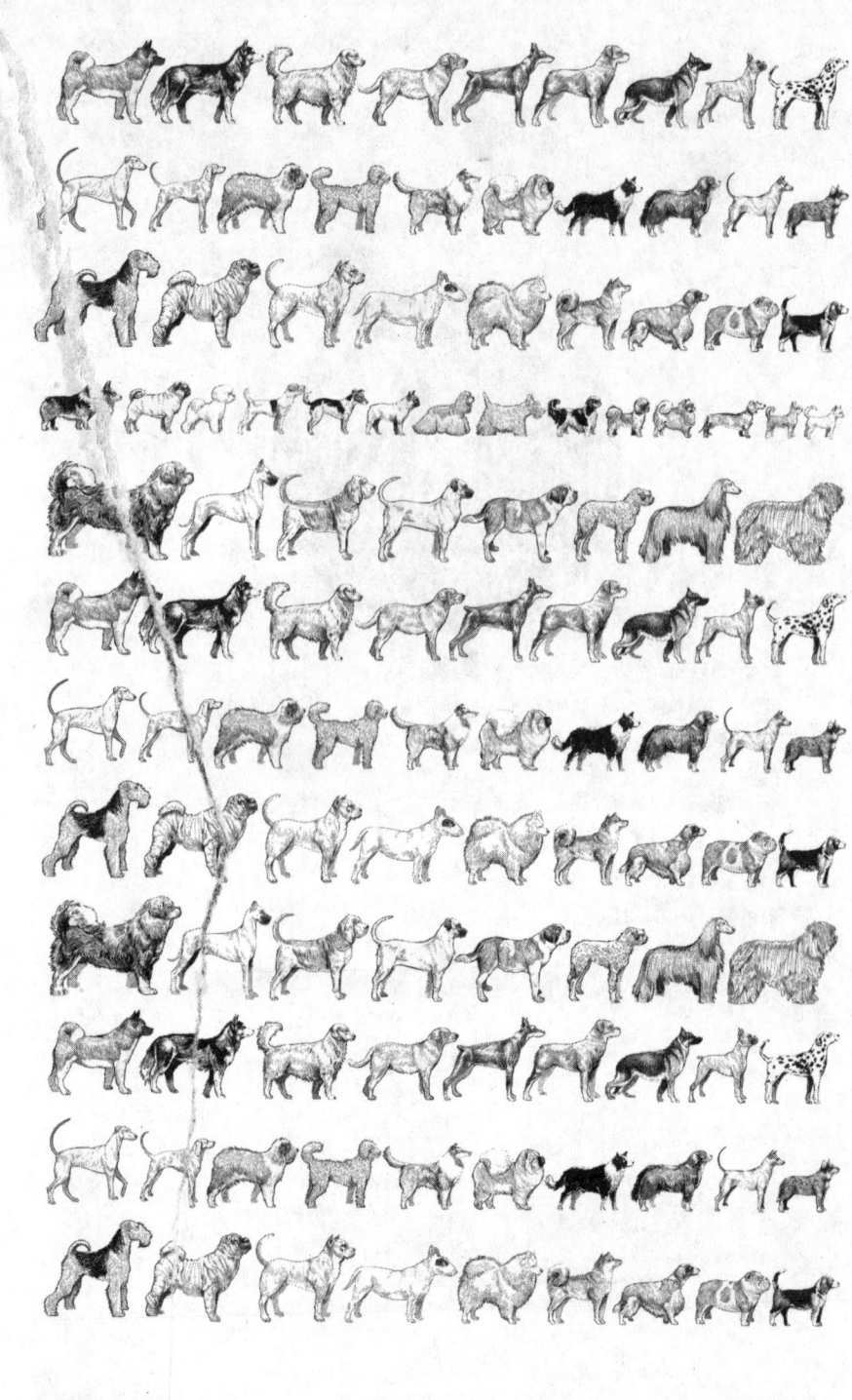

WOLF, MOON, DOG

• *a novel* •

THOMAS WHARTON

RANDOM HOUSE CANADA

PUBLISHED BY RANDOM HOUSE CANADA

Copyright © 2025 Thomas Wharton

All rights reserved. No part of this book may be reproduced, scanned, transmitted, or distributed in any form or by any electronic or mechanical means, including information storage and retrieval systems, without permission in writing from the publisher, except by a reviewer, who may quote brief passages in a review. No part of this book may be used or reproduced in any manner for the purpose of training artificial intelligence technologies or systems. Published in 2025 by Random House Canada, a division of Penguin Random House Canada Limited, Toronto.

Random House Canada, an imprint of Penguin Random House Canada Limited
320 Front Street West, Suite 1400
Toronto, Ontario, M5V 3B6, Canada
penguinrandomhouse.ca

Random House Canada and colophon are registered trademarks of Penguin Random House LLC.

The authorized representative in the EU for product safety and compliance is Penguin Random House Ireland, Morrison Chambers, 32 Nassau Street, Dublin D02 YH68, Ireland. https://eu-contact.penguin.ie

Library and Archives Canada Cataloguing in Publication

Title: Wolf, moon, dog: a novel / Thomas Wharton.
Names: Wharton, Thomas, 1963- author.
Identifiers: Canadiana (print) 202501252oX | Canadiana (ebook) 20250125218 |
    ISBN 9781039013964 (hardcover) | ISBN 9781039013971 (EPUB)
Subjects: LCGFT: Novels.
Classification: LCC PS8595.H28 D64 2025 | DDC C813/.54—dc23

Text design: Terri Nimmo
Interior images: (Le loup et le chien.) Ernest Henry Griset. From The New York Public Library; (running dog) Basicmoments, (space dog) Aimee, (multi-dog illustration) Rawpixel.com / all Adobe Stock
Cover design: Terri Nimmo
Image credits: (painting) Viscount Gormanston's White Dog (1781), George Stubbs / Artvee; (moon) H2Omanager, (running dog) Basicmoments / both Adobe Stock
Typeset in New Baskerville by Sean Tai

Printed in Canada

10 9 8 7 6 5 4 3 2

For Bailey, Boo, and Sam

*For he was of
the tribe of Wolf.*

MARY OLIVER, *Dog Songs*

Contents

WOLF

DOG

Rescue	45
Escort	51
Stick	64
Remedy	72
Bones	75
Banana	81
Beast	92
Good Dog	111
Go-Between	112
Underdog	120
Speak	130
Tracks	140
Scent	154
Breeding	163
Stay	171
Curriculum Wolfae	176
Laika: Stage One	178
Home	182
Wandering Cloud	194
Unleashed	198
Park	207
Moondog	215
Laika: Stage Two	219

WOLF

Part 2

Afterword	254
Acknowledgements	257

WOLF

The pack raced across the frozen lake in the moonlight. They were following no scent, chasing no prey. They ran because it was a night of frost and stars and the snow was thick and powdery and they were together.

Wolf stopped in his tracks.

His eyes had caught something on the far shore, among the dark pines. A bright flickering, as if the sun had risen too early and was hiding in the forest, unwilling to reveal itself.

When the rest of the pack noticed Wolf was no longer with them, they circled and trotted back to where he stood gazing.

What in World is that? Alpha asked as she came up beside Wolf. Alpha was their leader, the wisest and bravest among them, and Wolf was just Wolf. As the youngest and least of the adults he had no other name.

I'm not sure, Wolf said. I thought it was the sun.

Alpha's soft fur brushed ever so lightly against his, and Wolf felt his heart glow. She was quick and strong, and her coat was nearly all white, like the Great Mother wolf who lived in the moon. Alpha had led them well through the difficult days after her mate died in a fight with a cave bear over an aurochs carcass. It was only thanks to her that they had survived and stayed together. Wolf would do anything for her.

Wrong time, said Alpha. And the wrong place, for that matter. The sun doesn't hang around in the forest.

At that moment their noses caught the scent of burning wood. This was not the sun. This was something stranger. Trees only burned when lightning struck them in the heat of summer. They didn't burn in winter when snow was thick on the hide of World.

Quick shadows danced across the flickering brightness.

The fur rose on the back of Wolf's neck. There are animals in the fire, he said.

He ran through his inner checklist of hunters and hunted. Cave bear, brown bear, otherwolf, big cat, smaller but still scary cat, lynx, wolverine, fucking hyena. Deer, elk, bison, aurochs, horse, ibex, woolly rhinoceros, mammoth. Did any of them live in fire? No. Nothing that was alive lived in fire.

Alpha said, This isn't World but something else. It's not for us. Let's go.

She bounded off and the pack fell in behind her.

Wolf watched a moment longer, then he tore himself away and ran after them.

Wolf was alone as the sun rose, in a place of tall grass. There was no scent of his kind anywhere in World.

That could not happen.

Wolf panted, whined, darted this way and that, whined some more, pawed the earth. He raised his snout and howled for the others.

No answer. There was nothing else to do but run. Search. Find wolves. That was all that mattered. He broke into a headlong sprint and little birds shot from the grass with shrill cries. Nearby trees shivered in a wind that sang nothing about wolves.

Wolf ran until he was exhausted. At last he collapsed into the grass, panting, shivering.

Are you lost? something said.

Wolf leapt up and spun around.

An animal stood there on its hind legs. It was shaped something like a wolf but made of shadows, with hackles of bright fire flickering at its edges.

No, said Wolf, backing away. I'm not lost. It's the pack that's lost. I have to find them so they won't be lost anymore.

They're gone, said the animal. What it said was terrible, but its voice was soft and soothing. More like breathing than speech.

I'll find them, Wolf said.

You won't. You're alone. Come with me and you won't have to be alone.

The shadow wolf held out a paw. A strange kind of paw, without fur, without claws.

Come on, it said. Don't be afraid.

Wolf moved closer.

That's right, said the shadow wolf. That's it. Good boy.

Wolf woke. He was in the cliffside rock shelter the pack called home. Dawn was a faint reddening on the icy blue rim of the valley. Wolves were all around him, as they should be, stretching and nuzzling each other, preparing to head out into the promise of the day, to find something to hunt and kill.

His pack. His life. He was here with them.

That should have made him happy. It always had before.

Spring returned, soggy and blustery, leaving its muddy paw tracks on the clean white snow, which shrivelled and sank and disappeared. The low places filled with water and then clouds of mosquitoes.

Alpha's mate had died before the pair could make the spring's new litter of pups, and she had yet to choose a new mate. The beta male seemed the obvious choice, given his size and vigour in the hunt, but for reasons she kept to herself Alpha hadn't let him step into that role. Whenever he made advances she warned him away with snapping fangs. As for the other males, they didn't dare betray an interest in mating with her. With this lingering state of uncertainty about the pack's future, it was left to the beta male and female to deliver, and they got to work on it. One morning the beta female came out of her den under a ledge at the far end of the cave followed by six fluffy, toddling wolf pups who blinked in the dazzling new light of World.

Something was wrong with beta female, though. She was distracted and irritable, sometimes snapping at her pups as they nursed, sometimes batting them away. Eventually she crawled off alone into a hollow she had scraped among some thorn bushes. They heard her writhing and whimpering as if there were a fire burning her from the inside. Any wolf who tried to approach received a growled warning.

One morning they heard nothing at all from the hollow. The beta female's mate ventured in and found her dead.

From then on it fell mostly to Wolf, as the least of the adults, to keep a watchful eye on the pups while the others hunted. The pack ranged far and wide through the hills and narrow valleys, across the greatness of World, to find food for the hungry new mouths. For his part Wolf kept the pups out of trouble, while showing them what they would need to know to become hunters themselves. He taught them stalking games and wrestling games, and how to play tug-of-war with sticks and bones—all the skills they would one day depend on for their lives.

At last the pack wandered back to the dark lake nestled in the hills, where the prey herds had often been found in the past. Another wolf pack lived here too, one that they sometimes fraternized with and sometimes fought.

There were no herds. There were no other wolves. Instead there was a new animal.

It was the creature they had seen in the fire.

The new animals had established themselves not far from the water, on a rise above the pines and near a swift-running creek, with a view all around.

They were busy animals. And in odd ways clever, too.

They had constructed several small caves out of branches and prey skins and went in and out of them several times a day. The little caves were also where they slept at night.

And they kept fire, penned in a ring of small rocks. It leapt and smoked as all fire did, but it wasn't allowed to race out hungrily to eat World. It stayed submissively in its ring, warming the strange new animals and giving them light in the dark hours.

The new animals had done the unthinkable. They had made fire a member of their pack.

The new animals ate meat.

They ate berries and roots, too. Things the wolves ate only when there was nothing else available. But mostly they ate meat.

It was another reason they kept the fire. They burned the meat over the flames before they ate it. Despite this bizarre custom, the meat still smelled wonderful.

They're our competition now, Alpha said one wet and windy spring evening as the pack sat on a grassy hillside not far from the place where the new animals lived, watching them burn meat on their small, obedient fire.

Competition, scoffed Beta. Look at them. They can't run worth a damn. When they spot one of us they flock together and make all that jabber, like panicked ducks. They're terrified of us.

Since his mate had died, Beta had been making it clearer than ever that he was after the top job. He'd been standing up to Alpha, taking the lead on minor matters without permission, defying her in small ways that weren't quite enough to get him driven out or killed. It was plain to everyone that Beta was destined to become the new top male, but Alpha hadn't mated with him yet. The one time he tried mounting her she sent him packing with his tail between his legs. He'd been so humiliated he'd taken it out on Wolf, chasing him out of camp and giving him a few painful nips on the flanks for good measure. It was his right as senior male, but Wolf knew that with Beta this was more than pack tradition at work. Wolf was no match in strength for the bigger male, but he was better at noticing the unusual and at puzzling things out. Beta hated him for that.

I don't see the threat, Beta went on. They're just a new kind of prey we haven't figured out how to hunt yet, that's all.

They kill what we kill, Wolf said from where he lay, with pups crawling all over him and nipping at his ears. On rare occasions, usually when his betters missed the point, he dared to speak out of turn.

The rest of the pack stared at him.

They eat what we eat, he added.

So what? Beta snarled, baring his teeth at Wolf. There's plenty of food to go around.

For now, Alpha said.

What happened to the other pack? Beta wondered out loud one afternoon.

They were loafing on a warm, sunny slope across the water from the new animals, watching them go about their strange business. They hadn't seen any sign of the other wolves for days.

Look! Wolf said. That animal there, it's wearing one of them!

The new animal had a wolf draped over itself. Or something that had once been a wolf.

You still think they're prey? Alpha asked Beta.

Summer arrived, hot and rainless. The prey animals hadn't returned in their usual numbers, the great herds of aurochs and reindeer that poured over the bare hilltops and darkened the valleys. The few who did appear were mostly sickly and older. Not the choicest meat.

The pack was getting hungry. They spent more and more time hanging around the place where the new animals lived, observing.

The new animals had had better luck with hunting. They cloaked themselves in prey skins that helped disguise their scent. Their team tactics, like working together to drive a small herd over a cliff, were radical but effective. They also caught and ate animals—birds mostly—that the pack either couldn't catch or didn't bother with. And most astonishing of all, they had things resembling claws and teeth that they could detach from their bodies and hurl through the air to bring down an animal that was out of reach.

That's cheating, Beta declared, as the pack watched the new animals dispatch a lone older doe with their flying teeth. Prey the pack itself had been stalking.

Another day they found one of the animals' weapons. The tooth was a sharp, narrow piece of stone stuck on the end of a thin stick.

Longteeth, the pack named these things. With teeth like this now in World, a maw full of fangs felt quaint.

When they were finished eating, the new animals tossed away the stuff they didn't want: guts, wings, gristly bits, sometimes entire heads. And bones. Lots and lots of bones. They'd crack them open to get at the good stuff inside and then toss them away. On rare occasions they flung the leftovers far enough from their camp that the wolves would come across them during their exploratory jaunts.

Perfectly good bones, Beta said in disbelief when he returned from foraging near the animals' camp. Lots of good eating still on them. I don't get it.

A short distance from their camp, the new animals had scooped out a long, narrow pit in the sand. This, it turned out, was the place they went to drop and bury their shit. The wolves couldn't help but notice that the shit gave off the enticing greasy stink of the fine meals their neighbours were enjoying.

One night Beta snuck to the pit right after a young animal had used it but hadn't buried what she'd left. Beta was clearly hoping to impress Alpha with his daring. He returned unharmed to where the pack was waiting for his report.

That is some good shit, he said.

Beta went back the following evening for more, but one of the animals caught him creeping around and burned his rump with a stick that had fire on the end. He fled home yelping and trailing sparks.

A few days later a younger pack female was nosing around the bone pile when a flying longtooth tore one of her ear tips off.

We're moving on, Alpha announced the following evening when they had gathered at the cave. We'll go hunting somewhere else. These animals are too much trouble.

Are you sure? asked Beta. They have all those bones and shit.

And they have fire, Alpha said. You want more of that?

No, he said, his tail drooping.

And how about the longteeth, does anyone else want to feel one of those?

No one did.

Alpha had put her paw down. There was nothing more to be said.

Still, they lingered another day, and then another, waiting for Alpha to choose the right moment and give the signal. Everyone was hungry, and tempers were short. More than the usual number of fights broke out, and some turned serious.

Wolf got into a couple of scraps himself, one with Beta, who he knew could tear him apart easily if he chose to. Beta had started it by snatching a chunk of rabbit right out of Wolf's jaws. Before he could stop himself Wolf had let out an angry snarl. The next instant Beta was on him.

He won't kill me, Wolf thought as he writhed and rolled to get away from Beta's gnashing teeth. He's just putting me in my place.

But this wasn't a lesson in pack protocol. It was something more. Beta didn't relent, not even when Wolf tried clowning around, dancing and tumbling like a clumsy, excited pup. He was playing his role as the least of the adults, the kid brother who made them all smile and forget their grievances—and it usually worked. But soon Beta had Wolf pinned and was snapping at his throat, going for the lifeblood.

There was no choice but to fight back.

Wolf gave it everything he had and burst out from under Beta. Instead of fleeing as he usually would, he turned and barrelled into the bigger wolf, who wasn't expecting this rally. Wolf bowled Beta over and leapt on top of him.

To Wolf's surprise Beta went limp and bared his throat.

He was going to let it happen.

His fangs an inch from the hot blood pulsing through Beta's veins, Wolf hesitated. Then he climbed off Beta and flopped down nearby, casually licking his paws to make it clear he had no more desire for a fight.

Beta rose and gave Wolf a playful cuff on the snout as he walked past.

That was fun, he said.

He seemed amused, not angry or humiliated at being beaten. If he had been beaten.

It made no sense.

Wolf wandered off to spend some time by himself, as he often did. He'd had enough of the pack for now. As the sun slipped below the edge of World he sat on a high ridge and looked down at the firelight in the camp of the new animals. It danced gleefully, as if taunting him.

He wondered how these animals decided who would lead and who would follow, and if it all made sense to them.

In the morning the pack stirred early and got ready to head out. Wolf had crept back to the cave late in the night to find a warm spot among the curled sleeping bodies. In the promise of daylight, his uneasy feeling from the day before was mostly gone, and he was eager to be up and running.

Just a moment, Alpha said to Wolf as he trotted past her with several pups in tow.

Wolf halted and hurried back to her, his tail wagging happily. It stopped wagging when he saw the unquiet look in her eyes.

What is it? What can I do?

Alpha took a deep breath and looked away.

Beta came to stand beside Alpha.

Tell him, Beta said.

Tell me what?

Alpha said, I know you see it as well as the rest of us. There are too many of us and not enough food to go around. This wasn't an easy decision, but it had to be made. Someone had to be chosen.

And that someone is you, Beta said.

Chosen for what?

You're out, Beta said.

You can't mean that, Wolf said. That's not fair.

It's never fair, Alpha said.

Now Wolf understood why Beta had picked a fight with him, and why there had been so many other serious contests in the past few days. The lead wolves had been assessing who was essential and who wasn't.

Beta had let him win that fight, he realized. He'd given him a chance at a throat kill to see if he had what it took to help keep the pack alive in tough times.

He'd failed the test.

Let me stay, Wolf said. I won't eat much. I promise. I'll hunt better. I'll fight better. Let me stay with you.

In his distress, he was whimpering like a puppy.

You know I can't allow that, Alpha said. This is how it has to be.

That's right, said Beta. It's nothing personal. Now fuck off.

Snarls, snapping, and a couple of painful bites were necessary before Wolf finally slunk away with his tail dragging.

He watched from a desolate patch of tangled scrub willow as the pack bounded up the bare rocky hill above the old cave and into the neighbouring valley. At the top of the rise some of the pups hung back, watching him, yipping anxiously, calling their favourite older brother to hurry up and come along. When he didn't move they eventually turned and trotted after the grown-ups and out of sight.

He was alone.

His meals over the next seven days consisted of one mouse, one pocket gopher, and a few scraps of scaly skin and tiny vertebrae—all that was left from a fish that a bear had snagged in the creek and devoured on the shore. He even tried munching grass, like his usual prey did. An hour later he threw it all up.

He couldn't hope to bring down large animals without the rest of the pack.

Without the pack, he might not even be a wolf anymore.
So what did that make him?

His wanderings brought him back to the shore of the lake. Smoke was ghosting over the water from the camp of the new animals. Smoke that was rich with the scent of food.

Real food.

From a quick glance and a sniff, Wolf could tell that the animal was young.

It was hunched on a large, flat-topped boulder, so still that Wolf hadn't seen it when he'd come nosing around for cast-off bones. Then he'd caught the scent.

Wolf darted away to what felt like a safe distance. The animal didn't chase after him and didn't hurl any of those deadly long-teeth. It just sat there on the boulder, not even looking at Wolf, as if it couldn't care less what he did next.

There was a wonderful bone lying at the foot of the boulder, though. One that was still mostly wrapped in raw, bloody, gloriously juicy meat. The young animal had maybe dropped the bone by accident, or didn't even know it was there.

Either way, the animal was too close for comfort.

Wolf trotted away.

He came back the next morning.

The young animal wasn't sitting on the boulder.

But the bone was still there.

Wolf took it and ran.

The following morning Wolf returned, just to see.

The young animal was back on the boulder. And there was another of those wonderful meaty, unburned bones lying on the sand below it.

Wolf inched closer, nearly crawling on his belly. He licked his lips.

The animal raised one of its paws. A sound came out of its mouth.

Hello.

Wolf fled.

The animal was there the following day, too. And the unburned bone with meat on it still lay where it had been yesterday, unless this was a new one. It smelled of fresh blood, so it could be a new one.

Wolf crawled closer, wishing his jaws weren't dripping quite so obviously.

The animal made a gesture with its hairless paw that clearly said *Go ahead. It's for you.*

Wolf considered. This was a difficult thing to work out. The animal clearly didn't mind if he helped himself to the bone. But there had to be some kind of catch. You don't just give away food.

With a sudden lunge Wolf snatched up the bone and bounded away.

There was a bone for him the next day, and the next.

This is easy, Wolf thought. This is just fine. I'm in the pink.

The following morning the young animal was sitting on the rock as usual, but this time he was holding the bone in his paw.

A new wrinkle, and not a pleasant one. Wolf came as close as seemed prudent.

See this? the animal said with its paw, and then with its voice. It's yours.

Wolf didn't move.

You don't have to be afraid, the animal said.

I'm not, Wolf said.

Well, you're alone now. The others left you behind. That's hard.

I left *them* behind, Wolf said.

Either way, I think you've been enjoying these treats. This one's for you too. Really. No tricks. I just want to talk.

My kind doesn't talk to yours.

We're doing it right now.

I didn't start it.

No, but here we are.

What do you want?

I have this idea. Maybe it's stupid, but maybe not. I wanted to run it by you, see what you thought.

What's an idea?

You like these bones. So do I. And I like being alive. I assume you do as well.

Sure.

We'd both like to stay alive as long as possible. Agreed?

That's a no-brainer.

We actually have a lot in common, your kind and mine. We both hunt, we both eat meat, we have mostly the same enemies—those big scary cats and the bears and the fucking hyenas and whatnot. And we live with our families. Well, I do, and you *did*. Before whatever happened happened.

Nothing happened. I'm just doing my own thing for a while.

Okay. Well, that's another similarity right there. I like doing my own thing too. That's why I'm out here talking with you.

The point being?

The point being, you've got a terrific sense of smell and hearing—way better than ours. You can run like nobody's business, a lot faster than any of us. And those teeth. Yikes. But we've got the food, and all this advanced technology—the fire and the spears and such. So this is what I propose. You stay near our camp and alert us when anything dangerous comes around, and in return you can have one of these yummy jaw-crackers every evening.

Every evening.

Yes, and you won't have to hunt for them. We'll do the hunting. All you need to do is keep watch and raise the alarm if you spot anything we should know about. Anything that might be a problem. Like bears. Cats. And others like us.

There are *more* like you?

A few more. Here and there. They don't show up often. Some of them are okay, but others are bad. Really bad. They might not even be human.

What's a human?

That's what we call ourselves. We're the animals who walk on two legs and know things. I'm a kind of human called a boy. That means the bigger and stronger ones get to push me around and tell me what to do.

That sounds familiar, Wolf thought.

It also means I get to spend time alone, the boy said. No one bothers about me and I have time to see things. In my head. You know, like dreams. Things that aren't there. Sometimes I put things together with other things that aren't there, but could be. I call them stories. That's why we're talking now. Because I made a story in my head of you and me talking. Getting to know each other.

Okay, Wolf said tentatively, not understanding at all, and then he remembered his dream of the animal of fire and shadow. Ah, he thought. Things that aren't there.

Stories. He hadn't known you could make them outside of dreams.

The thing is, me and my pack, said the boy, we're the good humans. You never know about the others. They might try to steal our food and kill us. Not to mention all the nasty prowling things out there that want to make us their dinner. That's where you'd come in. You're good at noticing danger. You're fairly big and somewhat scary looking. You could probably drive a lot of the nasty things off just by, you know, doing your wolf stuff.

I could, Wolf said, puffing out his chest a little. It was the first time anyone had called him big and scary looking. Once he had chased a cave bear away from a reindeer carcass, all by himself. It was a small cave bear, not much more than a cub, really, but still.

So you're getting the picture now? the boy asked.

I think so.

You could put those skills to work, both for yourself and for me. For my pack.

Your pack?

Well, it would be *our* pack. We could team up, you and me. To stay safe and make sure there's plenty of food in our bellies. Basically I'm saying you've got the muscle and I've got the brains. Together we can make a killing. Lots of killings.

Killing is good. Food is good.

Yes. Yes. Good is good, but this could be even better.

I suppose.

Wolf thought of Alpha telling him he was no longer one of them. He thought of Beta saying *It's nothing personal.*

I get the bone first, he said, then I watch.

The boy pondered this a moment, biting his lip.

Okay, deal.

All right then, Wolf said. I'm willing to give it a shot. On a trial basis, mind you. And no tricks.

No tricks, of course, the boy said. That goes both ways.

Of course.

By the way, where did you learn to speak human?

I thought we were speaking wolf.

Oh. Anyhow, there's one more thing. You'll need to make some kind of big noise that's guaranteed to get our attention. What kinds of noises can you make?

Wolf demonstrated his repertoire.

He growled.

He snarled.

He yipped.

He yelped.

He whimpered and whined.

He howled.

Nope, those are no good, the boy said, shaking his head. Those are too *wolf*. They'll just bring more of your kind, and well, we don't really want more of your kind. One is plenty for now. On a trial basis, like you said. No, it's got to be a new kind of noise the other wolves don't do. A noise that'll mean something like *Hey, human, pay attention right now.*

Feeling foolish, Wolf tried out a few different sounds, most of which he'd had no idea he could make, until the boy shouted, There, that one!

Wolf made the sound again.

Can you do it any louder?

Wolf made the sound louder.

Okay, but I mean *louder*. Dig deep and belt it out.

Wolf dug deep and belted it out. To his surprise, it felt good. It was *his* noise. It was something new in World and he had made it.

That's it, the boy said, smacking his hands together. That just sets my teeth on edge. It's so annoying we won't be able to ignore it. Perfect.

By now a couple of the bigger humans had come running to see what all the ruckus was about.

Wolf bounded away.

Don't go too far, the boy shouted after him. Remember, *together*!

When evening came Wolf settled down near the edge of the humans' camp to gnaw the juicy bone the boy had left for him. He would keep his end of the bargain and watch. How could it hurt? He slept like this most nights, anyhow—fitfully, with one ear cocked for threats.

Nothing out of the ordinary took place in World that night. Some kind of night-flying bird Wolf couldn't see let out a few cries. A mouse scampered right over his toes and he let it, feeling indulgent. More than once the wind riled up and then settled down again.

It was all World and it was nothing new.

But there were other sounds and things to notice. Noises came from the humans in their little caves made of sticks and fur: snoring, grunts, drowsy murmurs, farts. One of the older humans came out of its cave to make water, gave Wolf a skeptical glance, and went back in.

Together, the boy had said. But in no way were they together. They'd just agreed to cooperate to protect the food supply. This wasn't even work. He might as well spend the night here as anywhere else.

Wolf felt drowsy and curled up for a quick nap. When he started awake he was still alive and the humans weren't in an uproar. That was good.

Still, he got up, paced out a few wide circles, cocked his ears, sniffed the cool night air. Then he lay down again for another nap.

At dawn the boy returned, but this time he didn't climb up on the rock. He approached Wolf slowly, and Wolf let him. The boy stopped a few paces away, closer to him than any human had been before. They looked out together at the dim grassy hills.

The night was over and nothing bad had happened. No one had been eaten.

Okay, said the boy.

Okay, said Wolf.

The following few nights were much the same. Once Wolf barked at what he thought was something large moving stealthily just beyond his range of vision in the dark. When the humans got up to investigate they found nothing, not even tracks. The older humans shouted at Wolf to shut his stupid yap and slouched back to their caves, grumbling.

The boy was the last to return to his cave. He nodded at Wolf.

Keep it up, he said.

Then came the night Wolf finally earned his bones. One of those terrible cats came prowling by. Wolf could see its eyes glowing like hot stones in the last of the humans' firelight.

The cats were solitary hunters, cunning and deadly. Even the pack was wary of them. In his experience the cats never spoke, as if it was beneath them to converse with another animal. Even when they killed they acted bored, like they'd rather be doing anything else. It wasn't enough for the cats to be terrifyingly capable killers, they had to be assholes about it.

The cat crouched in the shadow of a dead tree, not even deigning to glance in Wolf's direction, although Wolf had no doubt that his every breath and movement were being carefully noted. It occurred to him that his life was in real danger, and for the first time he was glad to have all those lightly slumbering humans with their longteeth at his back.

The cat stretched, licked a paw, and yawned.

It actually yawned.

He hated these cats almost as much as he feared them.

Wolf let loose. He made his new sound, louder than ever.

The cat started at the unexpected noise and then froze, dumbfounded. The look on its stupid, self-satisfied face, Wolf thought, was worth whatever happened next.

The humans came running with their longteeth and firesticks.

For a moment the cat stayed put, as if this pitiful show wasn't worth a tail twitch, then it turned and bounded away, with longteeth whooshing around it and thunking into the earth.

Several of the older humans stayed up with Wolf for the rest of the night, gripping their weapons as they silently kept watch.

They tossed him an extra bone, and one of them even grinned at him.

So you're not completely useless, the human said.

One night he sensed something moving stealthily in the dark past the camp. Several somethings. In another instant he knew—*wolves*.

Wolf held off making the new sound that would alert the humans. To his surprise he felt a feeling he'd never experienced before, inside where his heart thumped. It made him want to put his tail between his legs and slink away on his belly to some hiding place where no other wolf could find him.

He didn't. He kept stone still, hoping to go unnoticed.

No such luck. The wolf that was probably the pack leader parted from the others and came closer, sniffing, wary, curious. Wolf could see its eyes glittering in the light from the humans' dying fire. Wolf hoped it wasn't his pack and this wasn't Alpha.

It was.

She was still her shining, beautiful self, like a fall of snow in the moonlight. She made his heart leap as always, though he could see how lean she had become.

Evening, Wolf, Alpha said.

Wolf greeted her with a half-hearted tail wag. The sickening belly-crawling feeling was stronger than ever.

How have you been? Alpha asked.

All right, Wolf said, as casually as he could. You?

We're getting by. So, what are you up to?

Nothing much. Just hanging around.

This close to *them*? Wow, that's pretty ballsy.

They're sleeping. Not much to worry about, it seems to me. I thought you were taking the pack far away.

It was the boldest he'd ever been with her.

We travelled a long time, she said heavily. We searched everywhere. There was no prey. So we came back. The new animals have had better luck. Maybe it'll rub off on us. It sure seems to have rubbed off on you.

She looked pointedly at the well-gnawed bone between Wolf's paws.

I got lucky, I guess.

I'm glad, Alpha said. I wish things could have turned out differently.

Wolf didn't reply.

Well, fine hunting to you, Alpha said, and she loped away to rejoin the others.

The next night Wolf was on guard again, gnawing another juicy bone, when the pack returned, a whispering of grey phantoms in the grass. Again Wolf made no sound of alarm. As before, Alpha left the pack at a distance and came to him.

Still here? she said, sniffing.

It's a good spot, Wolf said.

Clearly. Lots of fresh food just lying around, waiting to be picked up. You wouldn't happen to know if there are any more of those bones hereabouts?

One of the animals must have dropped this by mistake, Wolf said. They're pretty clumsy and forgetful.

Yes, we've noticed. And you just happened to be nearby, like last night, to pick up after them. Twice in a row now. That really is luck.

Did you want something?

Only to say hello. But you know, I've just had the strangest thought. That you're . . . how do I put this? You're with them.

With who?

You know, *them*. The new animals. Like they're your new pack.

What? Of course not. What do you take me for?

I'm not sure, Alpha said. Then she turned and trotted back into the darkness.

―――

On the third evening he waited anxiously to see if she and the pack would reappear. If they were going to keep coming around, it increased the likelihood that one of the humans would notice, which meant they might also notice that he wasn't raising the alarm about it. And if that happened, his comfortable new livelihood would be in jeopardy.

When the pack didn't show up for several days Wolf figured they must have moved on again. He was relieved, but at the same time the truth of his new life hurt worse than before. It was like the ache of an empty belly, but worse.

Maybe, he thought, he should try making the annoying sound again, just for the hell of it. To remind the humans he was out here doing his job.

As he was pondering this idea he heard a sound and turned his head. Alpha was right there beside him. He jumped, nearly letting out a yelp. He hadn't heard her creeping up.

Easy, Alpha said. You'd better not be getting soft and careless out here by yourself. That wouldn't be prudent. Unless, you know, one has powerful friends to watch one's back. Then it might be okay to let one's guard down, just a little. I wonder, have you made any friends like that lately?

I don't know what you're talking about, Wolf said.

Yes, you do. We smell them on you. It stumped us at first, but we get what's going on here. You've landed yourself a pretty good gig. I admire that. I wish you well. The truth is, I almost envy you.

You do?

Almost. The jury is still out, let's say.

It's only on a trial basis. A temporary arrangement.

So what are they like, these animals?

Strange.

We gathered that much.

They're in World, like us, but also they're not. Not all the time. They dream when they're wide awake.

Really.

Yes. They spend a lot of time in these dreams, looking at things that aren't.

What's the good of that?

Wolf had a sense of how it was actually very useful, but the words were beyond reach.

I'm not sure, he said. They make plans.

So do we.

Yes, but just for today's stalk and kill or tomorrow's journey. They make plans for things you can't do. Or have never done. And then they do them. That's how they came up with the long-teeth. And the caves made of sticks. They take dreams out of their heads and bring them into World.

Maybe now you're one of their dreams, Alpha said.

This was an astonishing thought, and Wolf pondered it.

No, that's not it, he said. I don't belong to them. If it's a dream, then I'm dreaming them as much as they are me.

Well, that's a strange thing indeed. Whatever you've become, little brother, I think you're going on a journey with these animals to a place no wolf has ever gone.

She had never called him *brother* before. She had never acknowledged their bond.

He couldn't find words to reply.

I don't understand any of it, Alpha said, but I wish you luck.

You'll need it, said Beta's voice out of the shadows.

Fear shot through Wolf. The rest of the pack, or most of it, had silently crept closer and was now surrounding him.

The puppies weren't with them, he noticed. The new baby-sitter, if the pack had one, was likely keeping them away from whatever was about to happen here.

I told you all to stay back, Alpha snapped at them.

You're going to allow this? Beta growled. Who knows where it might lead, wolves teaming up with these animals. There can't be one of *us* on their side.

I'm not one of you, Wolf shot back, shocked to hear himself say it.

Well, you are and you aren't, Beta said. That's the problem. You're something that shouldn't be in World. You're a mistake, like a pup born with no legs, and there's only one way to deal with mistakes like that. The pack's way.

We're leaving now, Alpha said to Beta. We will leave him be.

Beta said, If you won't lead like a proper alpha, someone else will.

He lunged at Wolf, who scrambled backwards, but in the next instant Alpha was there. She collided with Beta and then they were tussling and snapping at one another. The other pack members stood motionless, as stunned as Wolf at what was happening.

In another moment Beta had wrestled Alpha off her feet and had her by the throat.

As the other wolves closed in on him, Wolf bared his fangs and prepared to fight to the last. Then he remembered the boy. He raised his snout to the sky and let out the noise, the new one, louder than he ever had.

The pack froze, confused.

Wolf uttered the noise again and again, until a hubbub of shouts and movement began in the humans' camp. Shapes emerged from the skin tents, dark shapes silhouetted by the fire. The roused humans and their long, sharp sticks were coming this way.

The pack turned tail and scattered into the night, led by Beta.

Alpha climbed unsteadily to her feet.

You need to get out of here, Wolf said to her.

Goodbye, little brother, she said. If we ever meet again, I'll be curious to know how things turned out for you.

Something came whistling out of the dark, struck Alpha in the side, and hung there. She let out a yelp and her legs buckled, then she bounded away, dragging the longtooth with her.

Early the next morning, a group of hunters set out from the camp.

Alpha's blood was on the earth around the spot where Wolf usually kept watch. He left that place and found a hollow under a fallen log, where he stayed hidden through the midday heat.

The pack didn't appear.

The boy did. Wolf heard him coming, by now knowing his footfalls from the others. The boy crouched before the hollow, a bone in his hand.

I've been looking for you, he said. What happened last night?

I did what I was supposed to, Wolf said. That's all.

Do you know those wolves?

I thought I did.

Well, I brought you something. In case you're hungry.

I'm not.

There were sudden shouts from nearby. The boy stood up and shielded his eyes with a hand.

The hunters are coming back, the boy said. My father's with them. I've got to go.

He dashed off to meet the returning humans. Wolf stayed where he was, but the hunters passed by not far from where he was lying.

Two of them were carrying Alpha, on a long stick. She was just hanging there.

Wolf scrambled out of the hollow and ran to her, tail wagging. In his joy, he forgot himself and trotted right up to one of the hunters, who brandished his longtooth and roared at him to get away.

Wolf sprang back and braced himself to help Alpha take down the humans carrying her. Then he saw it wasn't Alpha after all. It was only her head, with unseeing eyes, and her snow-white pelt.

Alpha wasn't there.

When the boy came looking for him Wolf trotted away. He spent the next few days out of sight of the camp, digging for mice and

voles, not really caring whether he caught any or not. He had no urge to eat.

He returned to the rock shelter that had been the pack's home. No pups scampered out of the den to greet him with their eager licking and pawing.

A howl rose in his throat several times as he wandered, and died before it could escape.

One evening Wolf plodded back along the shore to the camp of the humans.

The boy was standing on the flat rock, looking all around. Then he saw Wolf.

I hoped you'd come back, the boy said. Where did you go?

Wolf didn't answer. He lay down in his usual spot.

So . . . do we still have an understanding?

We'll see, Wolf said.

That night the full moon showed itself from behind a swift-moving pack of clouds. World turned silver. Wolf gazed up into the light, an anguished unvoiced howl trembling in his throat.

And then She was standing there before him, softly shining. The Mother of Wolves. He shivered all over, with terror or joy—maybe in her presence they were the same thing. He knew somehow there was no point in springing up to greet her in the rough-and-tumble wolf way. It would be like trying to tussle with moonlight itself.

Hello, little brother, she said.

It was the Great Mother, and it was also Alpha. Wolf gazed at her in fear and wonder.

Are you our mother now, big sister?

For you I am.

I didn't want any of this to happen. I just wanted to stay with the pack.

I know.

Are you taking me with you now, to the moon?

Not yet. Not for a long time. You have much to see and do here in World. I told you, little brother—you're on a journey that no wolf has ever taken.

I'm not a wolf. Not anymore.

As soon as he spoke the words, his breath caught in his throat and his heart went cold.

You are a wolf, Alpha said. And you always will be. I was wrong about that. This journey you're on—it's how the wolf in you will truly show itself, by facing whatever is to come and finding your way through it. As we wolves have always done. Though you will become something else, too, in time, something there isn't a name for yet, even if it's always been there too, nestled inside. I can't see all that's to come, but I know some of it will be very good indeed, even though these animals will try to make you into what they want you to be.

Wolf thought about the boy asking him to come up with a new sound.

I won't let them, he said

Well, you'll have an endless tug-of-war with them about how this pact between you is supposed to work. They'll make up stories about what you are, what you're for. Stories that will mostly be wrong. In spite of how stupid they'll prove to be about you, you'll need them as much as they will need you. You might even come to love them.

That's not going to happen.

Who can say? You have so many lives ahead of you. So many unlikely adventures. You might even forget there was a time they weren't by your side.

His every muscle drew tight, as if before a leap over rushing water.

I don't want to forget. I'm afraid, big sister. Please take me with you.

Not now. Not yet. At night, when you look up and I'm in the sky, remember that I'm guiding and watching over you. Always. So be brave, little brother, and be faithful to those you run with.

A great rolling shoulder of cloud moved across the shining face of the moon, and its light dimmed.

I have to go, little brother.

Wait, please. I have so many questions.

The silver light went out.

Alpha was gone.

The next morning the boy found Wolf and proposed they work together on a new project.

Wolf was going to say no, but he remembered what Alpha had said to him, and he agreed.

They climbed together into the windy uplands. The air was bringing Wolf the scent of the small prey hunkered down in the grass.

He scared up a lean, tawny rabbit and gave chase.

The boy tried to follow, but Wolf quickly left him behind.

Wolf ran and ran. The rabbit was fast but not fast enough. Wolf swerved and leapt at the exact right moment and brought it down.

The rabbit was hanging limp in his jaws when the boy finally trotted up, breathing hard.

That was something to see, the boy said, bent over with his hands on his knees.

Wolf dropped the rabbit at the boy's feet. He wasn't sure why. It just seemed the right thing to do while sharing a bright, windy day with someone. Share the kill. The pack always did that.

The boy took some human things out of the skin bag he carried and made a little fire right there on the hillside. He *made* the fire, Wolf marvelled. The boy cooked parts of the rabbit on a stick over the snapping flames and gave the rest of it, nice and bloody and raw, to Wolf.

Wolf devoured his share, then sat there licking his lips and waiting to see what would happen next.

After the boy finished his burnt pieces of flesh he stood up and kicked dirt on the little fire until it went out. He belched, wiped his mouth, then looked at Wolf, who had gotten up to stand beside him.

Good boy, he said, and he reached out a hand and cautiously stroked the fur along Wolf's shoulders.

Wolf shuddered. This was too much, too close. This was wrong—there wasn't enough space between them. No, no, no.

The urge rose in him to give the hand a nasty bite.

Then he noticed that the tail-drooping, belly-crawling feeling he'd had since he joined the humans was gone.

He liked the boy's hand on his fur. It felt right.

He wasn't sure what made him a good boy, since he was just being himself, but the not knowing didn't bother him too much. His belly was full and he *was* himself—he was still Wolf, as Alpha had promised.

They tried playing games, like fetch and chase.

Chase made sense to Wolf. Fetch, not so much.

He asked the boy, So why do I bring the stick back to you?

Because you want to.

I don't want to.

Just pretend you do.

Pretend?

They gave up on that and the boy proposed another game.

I'm going to go hide somewhere. You wait here. After a while, you come looking for me.

The boy started walking away.

Wolf followed.

No, no, the boy said. You *stay*. Right here. You wait. I'll go somewhere else where you can't see me. After a while, you come looking for me.

And then what?

And then nothing. You find me or you don't. That's it. That's the game.

The boy started walking away again. He looked back.

Stay. Right there. Got it?

Wolf stayed. The boy walked out of sight. Wolf waited. How long was he supposed to wait? The boy hadn't said. After a few minutes he got bored and followed the boy's scent trail directly to where he sat crouched behind a rock.

This is too easy for you, the boy said. Let's try it the other way. You go and hide, and I'll come looking for you.

And then I jump out at you, Wolf said eagerly, getting the idea at last. And tear out your throat, like a deer.

The boy stepped back a couple of paces.

You know what? Let's forget this game.

Just before dawn one chilly morning in early fall, Wolf and the boy were following otter tracks along a deep, narrow stream channel when the boy suddenly dropped to the sand.

Don't move, he whispered to Wolf. Don't make a sound.

What is it?

Remember what I told you about the bad humans? There's a pack of them just around the bend.

What are they doing?

They're crossing the stream in the direction of our camp, all crouched down and being quiet. It's a sneak attack on us for sure. This is really bad.

What should we do?

The boy frowned and stared straight ahead. Wolf knew that when he did this he was trying to herd his wild thoughts.

You run for the camp, the boy finally said. You'll get there a lot faster than I can. Warn everyone. If the bad humans spot you, they'll think you're just a wolf. They won't know you're with us.

Just a wolf.

You know what I mean.

What will you do?

I'll follow the strangers.

All right. I'm going now. Don't die.

I don't plan on it.

Wolf sprang to his feet, dashed across the water, and bounded up the far bank of the stream, headed for the camp. The human raiders saw him, but they didn't come after him or throw their longteeth. An instant later he reached the top of the bank and sprinted full tilt across the rocky upland.

In no time he was tearing into the camp, raising such a ruckus that everyone stopped what they were doing to see what was going on.

Danger! he huffed, too winded from his mad dash to form full sentences. Bad humans! Coming!

They understood. The hunters took up their longteeth and cudgels and hid themselves behind boulders and bushes.

When the attackers crept into what seemed an undefended, sleepy camp, Wolf's humans sprang out of concealment and charged.

Wolf charged with them and reached the bad humans first. He leapt at the leader, who was too stunned at this unexpected sight to raise his weapon. Wolf toppled the human and sank his fangs into the man's throat, choking off his cry of terror.

Hot blood spurted over Wolf's muzzle.

The other raiders froze at this unprecedented turn of events. Then they turned and ran.

Longteeth flew and two more of the bad humans fell. Wolf chased down another in a narrow draw and finished him, too.

It was over almost before it had begun.

They won't dare come back, one of the hunters said with a laugh. Thanks to our secret weapon.

I'm just glad it's on our side, another hunter said.

Wolf looked around wildly. The boy wasn't here.

He dashed back the way he had come, toward the stream. Then he pulled up. The boy was running toward him.

You didn't die, Wolf said, and he jumped up on the boy and licked his face. The boy stroked his fur.

I told you I wasn't planning on it.

That night the boy invited Wolf to sleep just outside the doorflap of his family cave.

Wolf approached warily and slept there. No one yelled at him or kicked him.

A few nights later a thick snow came down, early for the season. The air turned frigid.

When the time for sleep came Wolf crawled into the cave with the humans, imagining it had to be pretty comfortable in there with all those warm, greasy bodies.

Once inside he gave himself a good shake, snout to tail, to get the wet snow off his fur.

A yell and a thrown sandal, and he was scrambling for the door.

He curled up and settled into his usual spot. Through the night the soft, fluffy flakes fell and fell on his coat. After a while the snow became a second coat that kept most of his own heat close to him.

This wasn't so bad, he decided. He'd lived like this before, after all.

World made its turning and winter set in once more. The humans packed up their things and travelled downriver, following the herds to a more sheltered valley. Another group of humans were camped not far away, on the far side of a ridge. When the wind was right Wolf could smell their fires. Sometimes he heard them singing on cold, dark nights.

The boy explained that these humans were all right. His humans got along with them, mostly, though they preferred to keep some distance from each other. That was something Wolf understood.

The boy was almost full-grown. He was expected to go with the hunters now, after the big prey. To pull his weight, his father told him.

No more time for sitting on rocks, thinking up stories.

Wolf came along with the boy on one of these hunts.

The fire demon will give us away to the antlered and horned ones, one of the hunters complained to the boy's father as they left camp. We won't be able to get anywhere near them.

Fire demon? Wolf murmured to the boy. What's that?

It's what you are, the boy said. Because the spirits sent you to us, and you're quick and dangerous, like fire.

What are spirits?

I'll explain later.

I never have anything to do with fire if I can help it.

Quiet.

The fire demon has been learning our ways, the boy's father said to the other hunters. My son has been teaching it. It can help us.

One of the hunters laughed one of those disturbing human laughs with an unpleasant edge.

You saw what it did to the invaders, the hunter said. It's got a taste of our blood now. It's just as likely to turn on us.

He won't, the boy said. He can track better than any of us. He can sense the prey before we even see it. And he can chase the prey straight into our path.

Wolf whispered, Don't oversell me.

Well, you can do all of that. We've been practising.

Yes, but I never had an *audience* before.

The hunters grumbled but walked on. The day brightened. There was no prey to be found in the usual places, so they climbed up higher into the hills, where great slabs of rock jutted from the earth like immense teeth and the air was sharper.

The boy and Wolf followed, their steps synchronized.

Wolf's nose twitched. He stood still.

What is it? the boy asked.

Prey.

The boy silently signalled his father, and the hunters gathered around. Crouching low, they followed Wolf to the edge of a rocky outcrop. There below them was a small herd of ibex, grazing on the scant withered grass alongside a narrow stream that spilled from above.

The humans talked together in soft voices, making their plans.

The boy leaned close to Wolf.

Show them, he whispered.

Wolf slipped away, circling wide and low behind tangles of dead matted grass and tumbles of rocks, to approach the herd upwind and unseen, from a direction opposite to where the hunters lay hidden. He moved as slowly and cautiously as he could, but even so the ibex stirred, just a little—the twitch of a muscle running through the entire herd. A few raised their heads. They weren't ready to call a general alarm, but they sensed something was afoot.

Slowly, ever so slowly, Wolf crept closer and closer through the thin grass.

They call me fire, he thought. I'll show them fire.

When the moment was so right he could feel it humming in every sinew, he burst out of hiding.

Like one animal, the herd shivered, buckled, and bolted away, up the hillside in the direction of the concealed humans.

The hunters sprang out from the rocks and hurled their longteeth.

One of the ibex thudded to the earth. The rest swerved away from the humans, but Wolf was there at their heels, keeping them panicked, wheeling, unheeding, splitting into smaller groups, then into twos and ones. More longteeth flew and more ibex went down.

The rest bounded away, as if flying, over the crest of a hill and out of sight.

The hunters gathered around their kill, shouting and singing and clapping one another on the back.

The boy's father came to him, smiling, and put a hand on his shoulder.

Well done, he said, then he went to join the other hunters.

I suppose you helped, Wolf said to the boy.

Of course I did—it was my idea.

The boy's father returned with a bloody hunk of dark liver that steamed in the cold. He tossed it to Wolf, who tucked right in.

I thought of something while I was watching you, the boy said. The prey always stay together. Where one goes, they all go.

Right. So?

Well, it's one of those stories in my head. I saw the prey following us, staying with us wherever we go.

Prey don't do that.

No. But they might if you were there, making them go where we wanted them to.

Wolf pondered this.

I don't get it.

You're right. It's just a story. Forget about it.

On the way back to camp they met a group of hunters from the other human camp. When they caught sight of Wolf these new humans hollered and shook their longteeth. The boy's humans finally settled them down with gestures and calming words.

When the boy's father explained Wolf's presence, and how they worked together, the new humans asked, incredulous, It listens to you? It does what you ask it to?

We teamed up, the boy said, but his father waved for him to be quiet.

It was a gift from the spirits, the boy's father said. They sent it to us as a sign that we have their favour. Our hunting has been good today.

Where do we get one? the new humans asked.

You have to be patient, the boy said, but again his father silenced him with a raised hand.

Perhaps the spirits will favour you, too, the boy's father said.

Over the winter some of the other humans came to the boy's camp a few times in the evenings to share food and stories. On a few occasions the boy's humans were invited over to the other camp. The boy didn't bring Wolf with him on these visits.

They're not sure about you yet, the boy explained. Give them time.

Before dawn one morning the boy came to Wolf without his weapons.

I thought of something else we can team up on, the boy said.

What do you have in mind? Wolf asked.

It's better if I don't say too much ahead of time. Trust me, it'll be great. You'll see. Just go along with whatever happens and don't embarrass me.

I don't know what that means.

It means just follow my lead.

After the boy had carefully checked what he was wearing—something he'd never paid much attention to before—they set off.

Wolf followed the boy over a hilltop and down into the next valley. The camp of the other humans was nestled there in a deep draw. A few of the strange humans were already up and around, making fires and cooking food. As the boy drew near, the humans gave him a smile and a nod, but they eyed Wolf warily.

I guess they're still not sure about me, Wolf said.

Just be cool.

I don't know what that means either.

The boy led Wolf to one of the portable caves made from skins of the hunted and whispered that he should wait to one side of the entrance, just out of sight.

And then . . . ? Wolf asked.

Just lie down and keep quiet, the boy whispered. Then he made a soft sound, like a bird cooing.

After a moment the doorflap lifted and a girl came out of the cave.

You're here early, she said to the boy.

Oh, I've been up for hours. I always go for a swim in the lake first thing. Then I climb some trees to look for eggs. And then I check my rabbit snares.

Uh-huh, the girl said.

None of what the boy had just said was true, Wolf observed, but he thought it best not to comment. It seemed that being cool meant more of what the boy called pretending.

Do you want anything to eat? the girl asked.

Not for me, but if you've got any leftover bones for my . . . um . . . my . . .

At that moment the girl caught sight of Wolf.

Omygod, she shrieked, so loud that Wolf ducked his head and prepared to run. He looked around frantically for whatever threat had spooked her.

Omygod, he's beautiful, the girl said. They said you had one of these, but I didn't believe it. Will he let me pet him?

He will, the boy said, eyeing Wolf pointedly.

The girl squatted down to Wolf, and to his stupefaction she plunged her hands into his thick mane.

Omygod, you are just the biggest sweetheart ever.

Wolf glanced at the boy in alarm. The boy nodded.

The next unnerving thing the girl did was to cup Wolf's snout in her hands while she made kissing noises at him with her lips.

Mwah, oh, I love you, the girl said. *Mwah, mwah.* Who's a gorgeous guy, huh? Who's a gorgeous guy? You are. That's right. You are. Yes, you are. Yes, you *are.*

As if it had a will of its own, Wolf's tail began to wag.

I'm just gonna keep you, handsome, the girl said. That's all there is to it. Would you like to live with me? You'd like that, wouldn't you? Yes, you would. Yes, you would. You would like that. Yes, yes, *yes.*

Wolf agreed that this did sound like the key to absolute joy, but for some reason he couldn't form the words. His heart was turning mad circles in its bonecage.

The girl stood up.

Just a minute, I'll find him something, she said, and off she went at a trot.

Wolf started after her.

Don't, the boy said, toeing him in the ribs. Wolf lay back down, his head spinning. He'd lost sight of the girl. Was she coming back? She wasn't coming back. His heart throbbed painfully. He didn't know what he would do with himself if she never came back.

After a long agony the girl returned with a meaty bone. Wolf rose to greet her, tail wagging so hard his whole body shook.

Again the girl plunged her soft hands into his fur.

I missed you too, sweetheart.

She gave him the bone and he set to work on it. Meanwhile, the boy and the girl went off a short distance and talked for a while in soft voices. They joined hands too for a little bit. Then they came back.

You come see me anytime, gorgeous, okay? the girl said to Wolf. You're *my* boyfriend now and nobody else's. Got that?

Wolf gazed up at her with his tongue hanging out and his tail going mad.

Then it was time to head home.

Let's go, the boy said.

Wolf followed reluctantly. He kept looking back at the girl, who stood at the door to her cave, blowing him kisses.

They went back across the valley and over the hill to their own camp. Neither of them spoke the entire way. They could have been walking in their sleep.

Well, the boy finally said when the camp came into sight, you made a complete fool of yourself.

Did I? Wolf asked dreamily.

Oh yeah, the boy said. It was perfect.

They visited the girl often that spring. Then, for some reason, the boy stopped taking Wolf with him. Wolf would sit at the edge of camp, anxiously waiting. When the boy returned he had the scent of the girl all over him.

You sure you don't want me to come with you this time? Wolf would ask when the boy was getting ready to go see the girl again.

I'm good, the boy would say, and away he'd go, practically running. If he had a tail, Wolf thought, it would be wagging itself right off.

One day the boy came back from visiting the girl, dragging his feet, his head down, a scowl on his face.

He sulked for three days, avoiding Wolf, avoiding everyone, until finally Wolf cornered him at the shitting place.

Get lost, the boy said.

What's wrong?

It doesn't matter. It's over.

Over? What does that mean?

It means we're not going back there.

But what about *her*?

That's what I mean. It's *over*. Done. The end. Understand? We won't see her again.

What? No, that's not right. She's waiting for me. She said I'm her boyfriend.

The boy laughed, a sound that hurt Wolf in a place he'd never been hurt before.

Yeah, no, dumbass, you're not, the boy said. And neither am I.

But we teamed up on this, remember? This is a group project. You and me. And her.

Not anymore, the boy said. Now leave me alone.

A low growl rose in Wolf's throat.

The boy's eyes narrowed.

Did you just growl at me?

Wolf's ears flattened. The growl became a full snarl, with lips curled back and teeth bared. He hunkered down, ready to spring, or run. He didn't know which. He didn't even know why.

What's the matter with you? the boy said.

Slowly he bent down and picked up a stone.

Go on, get out of here, he said, readying to throw.

Wolf trembled all over. His voice had been seized by a beast that lay inside him, a beast without speech. He wanted to run to the boy, jump on him, bite him or bowl him over, show him it was just play.

I said go! the boy shouted, and he cocked back his arm and whipped the stone at Wolf. It hit a rock at Wolf's feet and flew over his head. Wolf shied, then turned and trotted away.

That's it, get lost, the boy said.

Wolf didn't look back.

This is over too! the boy shouted after him.

When the leaves came out again and the rivers ran full and strong, the humans took down their portable caves and began packing up their belongings. They were getting ready to follow the herds back up into the higher, colder lands.

Wolf watched them from a patch of berry bushes, staying out of sight.

He saw the boy working with his family, bundling things

together and putting them into baskets of woven twigs and bags made of stitched-together skins. More than once the boy set aside what he was doing and looked up, shielding his eyes with his hand, to scan the hills on the far side of the valley.

Let him look, Wolf thought. Let him wonder.

At last the preparations were done and the humans left the camp, walking in a long, strung-out line, carrying their possessions on their backs or dragging them on long poles of peeled wood they'd lashed together.

Wolf watched them walk away. Let them go, he thought. He would have the valley and the surrounding hills to himself. Unless another wolf pack—or something worse—staked its claim. Well, he would deal with that if and when it happened.

When the humans had vanished from sight he decided it was time to do something else with the rest of the day. He got up out of his hiding place and wandered the hills. He caught and ate a water vole. He chased a raft of ducks out of a slough just for the fun of it. Then the warming afternoon made him dozy and he lay in the grass on a windy hillside, letting the ever-changing scents of World come to him and make their music.

This would be his life then. Alone. So be it. He would make it work.

Alpha had been wrong about the path he would take. If she had been Alpha at all. Maybe she was just one of those things that aren't, that you meet in dreams. Maybe the humans themselves had only been things you meet in dreams.

There was one way to be sure. He could go back and have a look at their camp. If they had really been there, it occurred to him, if he hadn't dreamed them, then they might have left behind a few stray bones or other things worth eating. It was worth a quick look anyhow.

He trotted down out of the hills to the riverbank and nosed his way cautiously along until he reached the remains of the humans' camp. There was no doubting it: The grass was trampled down and there were a few discarded bits of this and that lying around, stuff of no interest to him. The human scent was still strong. It carried danger and something else, something even deeper. Something like what he'd felt when the pack left him behind. An ache in a deep place that nothing could reach.

Glumly he sniffed out a few shards of bone in the cold remains of a firepit. They were mostly charred and ashy, but there was some gnawing to be had. Wolf got to work on it.

He heard a rock move under a soft footfall.

His head shot up.

The boy was standing a few paces away. He wasn't carrying any weapons, only a deerskin bag slung over his shoulder.

Hey, the boy said.

Hey, Wolf said.

Didn't expect to see you here.

Well, here I am, Wolf said, and he went back to gnawing.

Yeah, so, I forgot something, the boy said. Had to come back for it.

What did you forget?

Oh, a thing. It doesn't matter. But since you're here, I have a thought. I mean, I wonder if we should maybe, you know, give the team-up another try. On a trial basis, of course. Only if you're interested. It's up to you.

Wolf hesitated. He thought of Alpha, and an immensity opened inside him, a territory beyond even his keen sight, where a wolf might lose itself. Or become something new. He understood now that she had been right, and he saw that if he crossed these few paces between himself and the boy, if he left with him and didn't come back, this time, he knew, it would be forever.

DOG

Rescue

Life, if life it could be called, found him posted at the doorway to the underworld, tasked with keeping living flesh out and dead souls in. Very strange, given that he also had three heads. Two would have made some kind of sense—one set of eyes looking outward for unauthorized entrances and the other set turned inward for escapees. But three?

One day he finally asked the queen about it. Once a year she was allowed to ascend from her gloomy throne to visit her mother in the world above. Unlike the king, who had put Wolf here at the doors and never bothered about him again, the queen would stop on her way out to see how he was getting along. No one else ever spoke to him. Her touch was as cold as a subterranean lake and she always looked sad, but she would pet him, scratch all three sets of his ears, and bring him bones from long-vanished monsters as treats, one for each salivating mouth.

Why three? he asked her. It was his middle head that dared the question, the apparently superfluous head, although it was the only one that bothered about such things.

The queen smiled that wistful smile of hers, the one that reminded him of an autumn leaf clinging to a wintry branch.

My sweet puppers, she said fondly, this lovely head right here—she scratched him between the ears—has the most important task of all.

He didn't understand, but she would say nothing more.

One day a man came to the doors carrying a lyre slung on his back. His face had been ravaged by some unspeakable pain, but the set of his mouth was determined. Unlike the shades that passed here on their way down to oblivion, this man was solid, warm, carrying the scents of earth and rain and sun-dappled meadows. The place above, that Wolf himself had come from as a pup. It was the first time in Wolf's watching that a living mortal had dared take this passage.

The outward-facing head saw the man first and shot up alert. Then all of him bristled. His muscles bunched and his three pairs of black lips curled back. A synchronous stone-cold growl rose in a trio of throats.

The man stopped, but didn't back away.

I'm going down there, hound, he said. I'm going to find her, and you won't stop me.

Wolf's response was to stalk menacingly toward him, in what any warm-blooded creature would recognize as the final warning before attack.

The man didn't flinch. He took up his lyre, softly plucked the strings, and began to sing.

Wolf's right head gnashed its alarming arsenal of fangs. His left head madly rolled its bloodshot eyes. But his middle head, against its own will, began to sway and droop. He had only one body, a single heart, and the music shot through it like shafts of sunlight through dark water.

She was my everything, the song said. She was my life. Where is she now?

Why? the song cried. Why did you have to take her?

Please, the song begged. Please, let her come back to me.

In the end all three shaggy heads softened and sighed, all three throats forgot how to growl. The song had unearthed a longing buried deep in Wolf that he hadn't even suspected, for something he had never known. He swooned, helpless before the music's obliterating power.

The notes grew softer and then ceased. The musician hurried past him, descending swiftly into the realm of shades. Wolf couldn't summon the will to rise from where he had sunk to the icy stone floor.

What just happened? his left and right heads muttered, groaning.

Later, to his shock, the singer returned from the depths, still living and breathing. It could only have been because his music was capable of charming even Wolf's pitiless master. Following the man at a distance came his beloved, little more than a pale shimmer in the dark. She was a shade, that was obvious, but as they approached the doorway she seemed to gain colour and solidity, as well as a warm, living scent, like the man's.

Wolf might have put a stop to this second trespass—the spell of the song had faded. But as they crept past him, stepping softly, he stayed where he was on the floor. There was no point, now that he'd already failed.

At the last moment the man stopped, turned his head, and looked back at his beloved. She halted and stretched her arms out to him, crying in anguish, Ah, my love, no! And then, like a blown-out candle flame, she was gone.

The singer called after her with broken shouts and sobs, and then he fled for the surface, weeping and cursing himself.

What was the point of anything if one mistake meant you lost it all? Wolf asked the gloom in anguish. Rising to his feet, he slunk away down an unused side tunnel and found a cleft there in the darkness where he hunkered. He knew full well he

couldn't hide forever. He would be found and punished. If you broke the rules you were always punished, without end.

It was the queen, shining like ice in the dark, who discovered him.

I had one job, his left head whimpered as she knelt beside him.

So did I, moaned his right. And I fucked it up.

His middle head sighed and said, I would let the musician pass again.

That's it, the queen said gently. Now you know yourself. That always brings pain. But you did well, puppers.

I did?

You'll see—the storytellers won't forget you. But you're out of a job, I'm afraid. Come along now, time to go.

This was it then. At least with her at his side the march to his fate wouldn't be quite so terrible.

Somewhere along the way, as she led him through the sepulchral grottoes and galleries, he noticed his left and right heads were gone. Had they ever been there at all? He wasn't sure, but either way he found he didn't miss them.

The queen was taking him upward, he eventually realized, not down. Where were they going? It had to be exile, probably in some forgotten shadowland where she—where no one—would ever visit him again.

At last they reached the doorway where he had failed in his trust. A new guardian stood watch, a true monstrosity with fifty heads, hissing snakes for hair, and a dragon's tail. If there was any dog in there at all, it was well buried.

Before she walked on, the queen had a pat on the head and a kind word even for this terrible thing. Wolf slunk past it with his tail between his legs.

The queen eventually led him out into the bracing air. He had been taken from the living world as a mewling pup, so long ago he'd forgotten almost everything. But now it all came flooding back. The bright god's chariot blazing in the sky, and green growing things everywhere, budding, unfolding, springing from the warming earth. The air moist with a thousand enticing bouquets that tickled his quivering snout.

He looked at the queen. What a change! She had a rosy blush in her cheeks and golden light shimmering in her hair.

She took in a deep breath and smiled.

Amazing what a little fresh air can do, hey, puppers?

They walked along a winding road for a long time, meeting no one, until they came to a gate in a fence. The queen unlatched it and Wolf followed her in and up a rising path that led between fields of grain and corn to a large villa on a hilltop with a bright tiled roof. As they approached, a pack of dogs came hurtling out of nowhere and surrounded them, dogs colossal and dainty, wiry and hulking, barking madly, darting, jumping, lunging. Larger than any of them, Wolf still shrank at the queen's side. At last he understood. He was to be torn to pieces by his own kind. That was fitting, he supposed.

Guys, the queen shouted, take it easy. Down, Titan. Hecate, behave yourself.

The dogs reined themselves in but continued to circle, tongues lolling and tails wagging. No, this wasn't threat or menace, it was a kind of dance he'd never seen before. They wanted something from him. What was it? Hips and shoulders bumped his and inquisitive noses sniffed his back end. He politely sniffed a couple in return. And then, without his being quite aware how it happened, he was inside a scrum of warm fur and toothy grins. Around and around Wolf and the other dogs whirled, nipping playfully and tussling, then they all flopped down together in the dirt, panting happily. Wolf's head spun. What was happening?

An older woman wearing a garland of flowers in her hair came out onto the portico. She and the queen embraced and shed glad tears.

You're early, the woman said.

I brought a friend.

I see.

The queen and the older woman sat on chairs under a sunshade, sharing a pitcher of wine and smiling indulgently as the romping kicked into gear again. The dogs dashed into the fields, and Wolf was with them, playing hide-and-seek among the stalks of grain. Together they flushed out a flock of irate blackbirds. They tore around the villa, flustering the goats and chickens. In no time, it seemed, Wolf had learned the way things worked in this pack and had a pretty good idea where he fitted in.

After a while he remembered the queen and padded up to her, giving her a questioning look.

Yes, she said, you'll be staying, puppers. This is your new home. These goofballs are your new family. You'll watch out for one another now.

His heart full, he trotted back eagerly to the others. He had been long enough in hell to know heaven when he found it.

Escort

The next time around, Wolf's home was a temple to the god of dogs.

It had its perks, being catered to and indulged as if one was a deity, or at least deity-adjacent. Each morning Wolf's attendant priestesses anointed him with precious oils and fanned him with palm fronds. He was fed the raw livers of ibises and mute swans, along with choice cuts from the hearts of gazelles. In exchange he had to sit still most of the day on a cushion, looking suitably semi-divine, while worshippers came and went making offerings to the god, whose giant jackal-headed effigy in stone stood at the end of the great nave. This was an endurance test, for sure, but it beat to hell the life of the strays in the streets.

Wolf knew there had been other dogs here before him—the scents left by the previous two or three hadn't entirely faded away—but he never bothered about what had happened to them. They'd had their moment in the sun. This was his.

———

Every ten days the temple icon-maker carved a relief image of Wolf in a block of soft clay. The clay would then be fired to hardness and used as the base for countless charcoal rubbings on stretched squares of cotton, which were circulated throughout the city by swift runners and put up on walls in public places, where people would gather to view the latest image of the jackal god's emissary on earth. They were encouraged to express their delight by dipping their thumb in turquoise ink and pressing it to the wall where the image of Wolf was displayed. When his life in the temple had first begun, a few dozen thumbprints appeared on the walls near each portrait. Now the new incarnation of the deity had captured the hearts of the people, and bright blue thumbs numbered in the thousands, all over the city.

He was a very popular dog. Or god. There was some ambiguity on this point, which was no real concern of his.

One day a shadow of grief darkened the royal palace. The young princess, beloved of the people and the joy of her parents, had fallen ill with a fever. The royal physicians burned medicinal incense, brewed potions, and inked hieroglyphs of protection and healing on her skin. Nothing helped. The red thread of the girl's life grew thinner every day, until at last the divine weaver took up her shears and cut it.

That same night the priestesses anointed Wolf with sacred oils and brought him to the necropolis beneath the palace. Here a priest directed him to be laid on a cold stone slab and his feet tied with ropes, ungentle treatment he was not accustomed to. He didn't have time to protest these indignities before the priest slit his throat.

He was standing on a plain of grey sand that stretched as far as his eyes could see. The sky above was the dim not-night, not-day colour he'd beheld in terror once when the moon passed in front of the sun. Only there was no sun here, or moon.

Near him stood a girl. Her eyes looked sad, but she stood tall and regal, her head raised as if in expectation.

Hello, dog, she said. Let's get to it then. We don't want to stay here any longer than we have to.

Get to what? Wolf asked.

What do you mean, what? You're my guide.

Guide? Says who?

She looked down at him with imperious annoyance.

It's what you were meant for, dog. Kept for. It's your job.

My . . . job.

Didn't they tell you anything at that temple? When a member of the royal family dies the temple dog accompanies them to the afterlife.

Are you sure there hasn't been some kind of mix-up? I've got a job already. I accept worship and I eat ibis livers for breakfast. We should go back. The priests can clear this all up and find your guide or whatever.

There's no going back, dog. These are the Tenebrous Sands. That means we're dead.

Dead?

Dead.

Wolf looked around. He sniffed. This place smelled like absolutely nothing at all.

All right, he said. Let's say we're dead. How does that make me anyone's guide? And anyhow, guide you where? There's nothing here.

Of course there's nothing here. These are the Sands, the wilderness of lost souls. That's why I need you. It's why they kept you in the temple. It's why you got the ibis livers. Your job is to take me to the Field of Reeds.

What's that?

It's where I will live for eternity, the girl said, and the sadness came back into her eyes.

Wolf's guts went cold. He shuddered, remembering the knife blade's flash as it fell. *Eternity* was a word the priests had used often, and now he understood what it really meant: The End. No more ibis livers. No more soft cushions or cool breezes from waving palm fronds.

Well, if he was stuck here, he'd make the best of it. The girl's destination sounded better than where they were now. Time to get moving.

Fine, Wolf said. The Field of Reeds. Any idea where we might find it?

If I did, would I need a guide?.

Right. Okay. I'll do my best.

Yes, you will, the girl said. Let's get going.

Wolf turned in a circle and sniffed. No direction seemed any less hopeless than any other, so he picked one at random and started off. The girl followed.

He dashed ahead of her, waited for her to catch up, and dashed off again. It was fun doing as he pleased for once, at least for a while. They walked and walked and nothing changed. Same gloomy sky, same endless grey sand. There was nothing to smell, to dig up, to chase.

So, this place we're looking for, Wolf said. A few details might help. What is it like?

Oh, the Field of Reeds, the girl said, and she began to speak as if reciting from memory. No more shall you bear your burdens or feel earthly pains. There, in those eternal fields, you shall walk among the swaying wheat, golden as the sun. Yea, you shall feast upon dates sweeter than honey and drink from deathless springs. In a sacred barge shall you sail upon the celestial river with the gods, basking in their divine radiance. Your days will be filled with joyful music and song, and you shall dance—oh, how you shall dance, child of earth, surrounded by the loving smiles of family and friends. In those fields your gardens shall flourish without toil or sweat, showering upon you pears and pomegranates and flowers of intoxicating scents. And when night falls—ah, such blessed nights—you will lie upon the bosom of the gentle, loving Mother and gaze upon stars brighter than any jewel in a monarch's crown.

The girl, it seemed, knew a great deal about a place she had never visited.

That sounds pretty good, Wolf said. How about the food?

Oh yes, the girl said. It is a place of endless abundance and bountiful—

HALT, boomed a voice like thunder. Before them, as if it had blinked into existence out of nothing, stood a giant scorpion. Its great segmented tail, with the ugly black barb of the stinger at the tip, rose over a head that ended disturbingly in the face of a woman. There was a stirring in the sand, and Wolf and the girl became aware of smaller but still alarmingly large scorpions gathering around them, like a living fence.

Who is it that comes before me? asked the scorpion woman.

The girl stepped forward and bowed.

O Lady Who Holds the Breath, she said, it is I, Esem, Princess of the Dawn, daughter of Semerkhet.

Greetings, Princess Esem, daughter of Semerkhet. You will go no farther until you answer my riddle. And if you fail to answer correctly, know that I will take your soul and it will remain with me forever, even as one of these.

The smaller scorpions crawled closer, their raised tails twitching.

Ask your riddle, merciful Lady, said the girl. I am ready.

A drum that sounds with no drummer, said the scorpion woman. A box of secrets without lock or key. A purse of treasure that holds no coin. I may be broken, yet stay whole. When I am given away, still I remain. What am I?

The girl frowned.

That's an excellent riddle, my Lady, she said. I thank you for it.

What is your answer?

May I think about it for a bit?

Take as long as you need. Time matters not here. Neither of us will be going anywhere until an answer is given.

The girl moved away from the scorpion woman and squatted beside Wolf.

Any ideas? she said.

Wolf didn't reply. He couldn't summon enough air to speak. Since the scorpion woman had appeared, he'd been helpless with fear.

Let's break this down, the girl said. What kind of drum has no drummer?

Wolf gave a pitiful whimper.

What's the matter with you? the girl whispered. You've got to get a hold of yourself or we're in big trouble.

She placed a hand on his shoulder. With the pressure of her touch, he was suddenly aware of the mad hammering in his chest. The girl noticed it too. Her eyes lit up.

She stood and faced the scorpion woman.

The answer, Lady, is a heart.

The scorpion woman smiled. Her massive tail uncurled and lay flat on the sand.

Very good, child, she said. Your own heart is valiant and resolute. You may keep on this road.

Wolf and the girl wasted no time. When the scorpions were out of sight the girl slowed down and turned to Wolf.

That went well, she said. Anyhow, we must be going in the right direction, since we've passed the first of the trials.

Wolf halted.

The *first?*

An unguessable amount of time later they came to a wide, swollen river where a huge crocodile with a disquieting grin and far too many teeth lay basking on the shore, surrounded by rows and rows of small black stones. The crocodile offered to carry them across on his back, but only if the princess surrendered to him the thing she most wished to keep. If she refused, he would swallow her up and her soul would be shat upon the sands as a stone, to lie here with all the others for eternity.

O mighty Lord of Waters, I brought nothing with me, the girl said. Not even my clothes.

What you most wish to keep, the crocodile said, is not a thing you carry or adorn yourself with. It lies in the deepest part of you.

Again the girl asked for time and squatted beside Wolf, who was trembling again and trying to make himself as small and inconspicuous as possible.

It can't be my heart, she said. We already answered that. Plus I'm going to need my heart when I get to the Field of Reeds, to prove I'm worthy. What do you think, dog? What do you have that you would never want to give up?

It used to be my life, Wolf said, transfixed by the crocodile's huge teeth, which still had gobbets of its last meal wedged between them. But I guess I've already lost that.

All right, other than your life, what meant more to you than anything else?

Wolf was about to answer *food*, but he hesitated. A memory had leapt to mind, forgotten until this moment. He saw the face of one of the priestesses who had tended him. Her name was Bala. She had been captured in a war far to the south and brought against her will to serve at the temple. And to service the priests, it seemed, judging by the pitiful cries he heard when she was summoned to their chambers at night. After one of these summonings Bala had crept to Wolf's sleeping place, weeping quietly. She had called him a good boy and taken him in her

arms and held him until her tears stopped. No one else at the temple had ever held him or spoken kindly to him. One did not become familiar with a sacred animal. That was forbidden.

I remember—he began, then stopped.

Yes, go on, the girl said encouragingly. You remember?

Never mind. I was just thinking of somebody.

Someone you loved?

No. I don't know. I mean, I wish . . .

The girl patted him on the shoulder.

That's it, dog, she said.

She turned and faced the crocodile.

O Lord of Waters, more than anything I want to be back home, she said. With my mother and father and brothers and sisters. But I can't be.

So what do you surrender?

I don't know what to call it. It's not a thing I wish to keep. It's the wanting to keep it. To keep anything. That's what I offer you.

Very good, the crocodile said, his grin widening. Your payment is acceptable. I will carry you across.

Despite Wolf's misgivings, the crocodile was as good as his word.

On the far shore a road paved with great flat stones wound among low hills. Encouraged by this new development, Wolf and the girl quickened their pace.

A vague amount of time later they came around a bend to find that the road ran onto a narrow bridge that arched over a deep chasm. They walked onto the bridge, trying not to glance over the sides into the bottomless deeps.

At the height of the bridge stood a low table of stone with a small wooden object on it. On the far side of the table, on top of a squat urn, a large black cat lay curled. She wore a collar of gold and, like a human, she had long hair plaited in thick braids.

Wolf halted and bristled, but the girl kept on.

Welcome, the cat said, rising. She lifted a paw and gestured to the table. Would you care to play a game with me?

They could now see that the object on the table was a narrow wooden board dotted with holes. Slender pieces of ebony and ivory, like nails with carved heads, stood in holders, the black all gathered at one end and the white at the other.

Hounds and Jackals, the princess said with a laugh. I played this all the time with my father. I beat him just about every time. It's a fun game, but I would really rather just keep on, if that's all right with you, O great Protector and Devourer.

It's not all right, I'm afraid, said the cat. If you wish to cross the bridge, you must play. And you cannot go back.

I thought you might say that, noble Benefactress of the Household. Very well.

The girl sat down cross-legged at the near side of the table.

One more thing I should mention, the cat said. You are required to play, but you must not lose or win. Either outcome shall see you cast into the abyss below, where your batlike soul will flutter about the netherworld forever in lamentation.

The girl went pale.

But . . . there's no stalemate in Hounds and Jackals. There can't be a draw. You either win the game or you lose.

Just so.

Fine. Let's begin. Shall I play hounds or jackals?

I leave that to you, the cat said.

The girl looked back at Wolf, who stood rooted to the spot.

I'll choose hounds, she said, and picked up one of the white pieces.

Wolf gave in and sat on his haunches at the girl's side. The game began. The girl moved a piece. The cat moved another. Back and forth they went. Wolf's eyes darted between the players and the game pieces. The priests at the temple had spent hours at this strange activity, which had never made any sense to him.

As the match progressed it became clear even to Wolf that the girl was having difficulties. As the black and white carven nails went up and down the board she pursed her lips, drummed the table with her fingers, grimaced, sighed, wiped her brow. It began to take longer and longer for her to move one of her pieces. Finally she sat hunched over the board without moving at all, her teeth gritted and her hands in fists in her lap.

Your turn, the cat purred, its long tail swishing slowly. Wolf felt a sudden murderous urge to lunge across the table and put this smug feline in her place. He restrained himself, sensing the futility of fangs and claws here.

The girl stared at the board, her brow furrowed. Then she leaned down and scratched Wolf under the chin.

This isn't going well, she whispered in his ear. I'm one turn away from winning, but I dare not make the move. But if I don't, she finishes me on her next turn. I can't see a way out of this where we don't end up down *there*. If you've got any insights, now's the time.

Wolf cocked his head and studied the slender pieces with their carven heads. He took a few careful sniffs and even licked the edge of the wooden board.

Defeated, he slumped down.

I don't get it, he said. They're all just dogs.

The girl blinked. She looked back at the board.

Without a word, she picked up one of the cat's jackals and moved it into an empty space.

The cat's eyes narrowed and her tail lashed back and forth.

What do you think you're doing? she hissed. That is not your piece.

It's not yours, either, mighty Slayer of Rats and Serpents. In this place there are no hounds or jackals anymore. No black and no white. No masters or slaves walk this road, no kings or beggars. There's no longer any game to win or lose.

A taut silence hung over the board. Then a green gleam lit the cat's eyes.

Very wise, child. Well played indeed. You may pass. You've won something far more valuable than a game today.

On the far side of the bridge the road continued. They followed it and came to a wall of stone that stretched away in either direction until it was lost from sight. In the wall was a gate in the shape of a scarab's wing case, lit darkly with shirrs of iridescence. A tall human sat by the gate on a low stool, a staff in his hand with its head carved in the shape of an animal Wolf couldn't identify. The human himself had the narrow regal head of a jackal. Or perhaps he was wearing a mask. It was difficult to tell.

Mortal child, this is the gate to the Field of Reeds, the jackal-human said. You have passed the trials and your heart has been weighed and found worthy. You may enter now and take your place among the immortals.

The gate's scarab-wing doors stirred and swung open. Beyond, the princess could see a broad avenue between stands of tall, waving reeds, as expected, leading to a dappled countryside of grain fields and orchards. Beyond that, on the wide, calm surface of a river, boats with golden sails gleamed in the sun.

Oh, she breathed. It's even more beautiful than I imagined. I can smell lotus flowers like the ones we had in the bathing pools back home. And the honey cakes that Grandmother used to bring me. I can hear children playing and the tamed birds singing in their cages.

Head high, she strode across the threshold, gazing in rapture at what lay before her.

Wolf remained just outside the gate. When the doors had opened he'd beheld nothing on the far side but more grey sand, without scent or sound of any kind. Whatever the girl could see and sense, he could not.

When she realized she was walking alone she stopped and turned.

Come, dog, she said.

Wolf didn't move.

He cannot join you, the jackal-man said.

Why not?

This is not his eternal reward, the jackal-man said. It is yours.

That's not fair. He went through everything I did to get here. He's mine now. Come here, dog.

Wolf remained still and silent.

Why don't you speak? the girl said. Say something.

You have gone where he cannot go, the jackal-man said. Your fates are sundered now, as is your speech. His destiny lies elsewhere.

I see, the girl said. For an instant her eyes softened.

You have my thanks, dog, she said. May the gods be kind to you.

The gates swung shut and the girl vanished.

Wolf and the jackal-man regarded one another.

So . . . now what? Wolf asked.

You have done well, cousin, the jackal-man said, and you shall be rewarded. It is in my power to return you to the living.

Really? I can go back?

You may be reborn as a dog, yes. There is no certainty, however, of the easy life you once knew.

Well, if my life always ends this way, I'm fine with that.

So you say. But know that you might end up the dog of a master who wields a whip rather than kind words. And your end might come sooner and be harsher, used up in pulling heavy carts or turning spits in stifling kitchens. Or worse. Believe me, cousin, there is much worse, for a dog. But as I find your heart worthier than most, I offer you another choice. You may take new breath as a human, and thus gain the precious opportunity to be rewarded one day with a forever home.

Honestly, it doesn't look like much to get excited about.

To one of your kind it would not. It is a place for human souls.

No fleas there?

No fleas.

All you can eat?

Of course.

And I wouldn't be a dog.

No, you would not be a dog. Forever. So, what do you choose?

Stick

Look at that worthless, flea-bitten cur, the passersby said, shaking their heads. Lounging around in the sun, doing nothing useful.

They weren't talking about Wolf but about the human he kept company with in those days, a philosopher who lived on the streets like a beggar and whom everyone called the Dog.

Yes, I'm a dog, the philosopher would say to anyone who flung the name at him as an insult. I love the good, bark at the unkind, and bite the wicked.

It was the barking he excelled at. The Dog was notorious for lobbing harsh words at anyone he felt needed them.

Most people go through life asleep, he said. This is how I wake them up. You can't teach anyone anything with niceness. It lets them off the hook.

The philosopher's most frequent habitation was a large clay storage jar, tipped on its side in a sunny corner of the agora. During bad weather, there was just enough room inside the jar for dog and human to curl up together and keep warm. For every townsperson who mocked the philosopher and spat at him, there was another who came respectfully to hear his teachings, and these visitors often left food in thanks. Food that the philosopher happily shared with Wolf, who had started hanging around the jar one day and never left. The visitors would sometimes comment on how lucky this scruffy little mongrel was, out of all the strays that infested the town, to find this gig as the companion of a wise man.

The truth was, the Dog had gotten most of his ideas from Wolf.

From Wolf's lack of possessions the philosopher had learned the value of owning nothing and making do with whatever leftovers and cast-offs came his way. When someone mocked or threatened him he was ready with a sharp retort. He pissed and shat in public and pleasured himself in front of whoever happened to be walking by. He often said he wished he really was a dog so he could lick his own balls.

If you want to live a good life, he maintained, follow Nature.

When asked for specifics he would gesture to Wolf, lying beside him in the sun, and say, Take this lazy mutt as an example. He idles away his days without shame or remorse, accepting with a shrug whatever life brings. And he's happy. The happiest creature I know. If you wish to live like that, start by giving away what's hanging around your neck and weighing you down. House, possessions, wealth, friendships. Dump it all. Shun society and its hypocrisies, forget ambition and fame, and you will walk as a free man among the chained.

Usually the humans who asked the question would thank the Dog and walk away sadly, knowing they didn't have the courage to follow such a hard road.

What is so wrong with wealth? a rich young nobleman once asked. He and his companions were infamous for marauding drunkenly around town, picking fights and causing mayhem. They had stopped to fling taunts at the philosopher, and a crowd, anticipating some entertainment, had quickly gathered around them. The Dog said nothing in reply to their japes and gibes. He sat there lazily scratching his armpits.

Look at me, all of you, the young nobleman said, raising his arms and turning in a circle. Look at my fine robes and jewelled sandals. I have a beautiful house with an army of servants. I have a smoking-hot mistress, a ready purse always full of cash, and the fastest horses in town. Admit it, I have the life you all wish you had. Even this big phony sitting here making a virtue of his dirt and sores secretly envies me. What do you say to that, Dog?

The philosopher left off scratching his armpit, lifted a buttock, and farted.

The crowd tittered and guffawed.

The young nobleman's face turned even more scarlet than drink had already made it. He roared, lunged forward, and kicked the Dog in the face. Wolf jumped up, barking madly, and the nobleman's friends leapt in, ready with the cudgels they had concealed beneath their cloaks.

In a few moments it was over. Wolf and the Dog lay on the stones, bruised and barely able to move. The young men walked off, laughing and slapping each other on the back. With the show over, the crowd dispersed.

The Dog spat out a tooth.

Fuck them, he said.

It wasn't the first time something like this had happened and it likely wouldn't be the last. With the Dog, philosophy was a full-contact sport.

It might be time, Wolf reflected, to move on.

Still, he stayed. While he had been instructing the Dog on the good life, he had also been honing his own philosophy.

Each morning he and the Dog woke at the same time. They

would both scratch themselves in various itchy places, the philosopher would absently pet Wolf and, just as absently, Wolf would lick his hand. Then they would get up and begin their day.

The philosopher would take an early walk around the agora, which was just beginning to stir. Wolf would accompany him, nose to the ground, snuffling out whatever trampled scraps and tidbits might be left from yesterday's commerce. He usually came across something—a heel of bread, a squashed olive or two, an apple—that a human who wasn't too picky would find edible, and right away the philosopher registered the change in Wolf's stance and realized there was something there for him, too. Or, with his upright stance, the philosopher might spot something of interest that wasn't visible to his companion, and Wolf would follow his gaze and investigate.

The Dog never put Wolf on a leash. He always said he was no one's master, that he and the animal were companions who had chosen one another freely. And anyhow there was no need to leash Wolf. He was clever enough not to be the kind of nuisance that someone ended up strangling.

When the sun grew too hot Wolf knew the philosopher would seek a shady spot, and by the scent of leaves and the sound of birds he would lead him to a suitable one. When the days were cold the philosopher would shelter in a temple portico where a brazier always burned. Worshippers often dropped a coin or two in the Dog's palm, to show the resident deity how generous they were to the unfortunate. Wolf could always tell which passersby were susceptible to appeals, and when those humans crossed the portico he would wag his tail and look as harmless and in need of charity as possible.

Sometimes Wolf found a good-sized stick and the Dog could be coaxed into playing fetch. When the philosopher got ready to throw the stick, Wolf predicted its trajectory from the way his arm tensed and cocked, guessing where the stick would land even before it left the human's grasp. To keep the game exciting, the philosopher would sometimes suddenly change the direction and force of his throw, and when Wolf returned with the stick he sometimes darted away, refusing to give it up.

This flow of anticipation, response, and surprise left them both smiling.

On those rare occasions when the philosopher had access to papyrus and pen to scribble out his ideas, Wolf would lie at his feet. His quiet presence anchored and steadied the philosopher so that his thoughts were less likely to dash in mad directions and chase their own tails. Wolf, in turn, was soothed by the steady scratching of words he had no need to read for himself.

When someone came by seeking wisdom from the Dog, Wolf would lounge at his ease nearby, usually with his nether parts on full display, a living exemplum of Nature in all its innocence.

Their day was like a dance, each move made around and with the other. So they went through life, usually without a single word needing to be spoken.

Together, Wolf had come to understand, they were more than each could be alone. They might even, he speculated, be one thing.

If he had been given to philosophical jargon, Wolf might have called this his theory of transspecies intersubjectivity. He sometimes considered sharing his ideas with the Dog, but lately he'd been finding it more and more difficult to actually talk with humans. They were so caught up in their own affairs they didn't seem to hear him anymore when he spoke. Anyhow, it never seemed to be the right time to broach the subject. Why struggle for a way to describe what you lived and breathed in every atom of your being? (They had both learned about atoms from Democritus).

One day a visit from the young conqueror—the boy king that everyone was hailing as *the Great*—had the town in an uproar.

He met first with the assembly of leading citizens and received their pledge of fealty. The city's philosophers came to pay their respects to the glorious hero as well. All but one.

The young conqueror waited patiently as his new subjects grovelled. Then he assured them they could carry on with this foolish fad called democracy, as long as they did whatever he told them to. When that business was finished the citizens begged to know what else the young conqueror might wish for while he graced them with his august presence.

There was only one other thing he wanted: to meet the infamous freethinker known as the Dog.

The leading citizens hurriedly escorted the young conqueror to the agora, where they found the philosopher lying in front of his jar, soaking up the sun, with flies buzzing around him. Wolf lay at his side, drowsing in the heat.

The conqueror approached. His shadow fell over the philosopher, who opened his eyes and blinked. Wolf snapped awake too. Something unusual was taking place—he could feel it in the way the citizens stood bunched and cowering behind this golden-haired human in gleaming leather armour, whose bronzed skin glinted with the dust of strange lands.

I've come to speak with you, the young conqueror said to the Dog, if you will spare me the time.

The citizens exchanged looks of wonder at the humility shown by this shooting star of a youth, who had already blazed across entire kingdoms and showed no signs of slowing down. They knew he had been schooled by Aristotle and had learned to revere deep thinkers, but still they hadn't expected such deference toward their own mangy, annoying know-it-all.

As for the Dog, he didn't rise or prostrate himself. He just sat there blinking like an idiot at the world-shaking colossus towering over him.

I find your ideas intriguing, the young conqueror said. And refreshing. I'd like to know how someone like me, with so

many cares of state and of war, might put them into practice. I'm not asking from idle curiosity but with a sincere desire for instruction.

The Dog scratched his beard and said nothing. Wolf caught the tension in the crowd, their silent urging that the philosopher at least mumble a deferential word or two before his insolence brought disaster down on all their heads.

Well then, said the young conqueror, apparently not put out by this rudeness, might I ask if there is anything I can do for you, a great thinker of such renown.

You can stand out of my sunlight, said the Dog.

Gasps and squeaks of fear came from the citizens. One of them fainted and several backed away, preparing to run.

The conqueror laughed heartily.

Of course, he said. Forgive me.

He moved to let the sunshine fall on the Dog once more. Then he turned his attention to Wolf.

This is a fine hound, he said. What do you call him?

I don't call him anything, the Dog said. He doesn't have a name for me either. We get along fine that way.

Well, since he seems as well suited to the wandering life as a philosopher, or a soldier for that matter, I will name him Peritas. Where did you find him?

We found each other, the Dog said. I don't own him and he doesn't own me. He may do as he pleases.

Is that so? the young conqueror said, squatting down in front of Wolf, to the shock of the assembled townsfolk. Then how would you like to come travel with me, noble Peritas? I'm going to conquer the whole world.

Had it been anyone else, Wolf would likely have ignored such a ridiculous—not to mention condescending—come-on. They had only just met, after all. But he could feel the power emanating from this strange human, the irresistible, supernatural charm. He recognized it right away.

The young conqueror was a stick.

The grandest, shiniest, most irresistible stick in the world, one you couldn't help chasing but would never catch. And the fawning humans clustered around him were the dogs who ran after this marvellous stick wherever it flew. They would throw their lives away just to get close to this glorious golden stick, to have its favour and bask, even for a moment, in its radiance.

Who could say no to the sun? The scent of remote empires and barbaric airs that wafted from this magnificent human called to a part of Wolf he hadn't even known was there.

Life was fine here with the Dog, but what more could life be?

Wolf leapt up on the young conqueror, pawing him and wagging his tail excitedly.

I thought you might say yes, the golden youth said, laughing. Very well then, let us begin our wanderings together, Peritas. You and I, to the ends of the earth.

As if he had already forgotten the philosopher he had asked to meet, he strode away, with a train of baffled citizens in his wake.

Wolf hesitated and turned for one last look at the Dog. In a single mad instant he had tossed aside their unspoken pact, their mutual esteem and understanding, and for what? Glamour and glory, chimeras the two of them had always scorned. He was betraying everything he and this human had been to one another, and he was doing it with joy in his heart.

But after all, wasn't this Nature too? Wasn't this obeying what you really were?

Go on, the philosopher said, with a grin missing several teeth. I might have done it too, if I wasn't such a lazy dog.

Remedy

When did you first start feeling this way? the healer asked, holding the back of his hand to the man's forehead. They were seated facing each other on a rug of woven maguey leaves in the healer's hut. Grey mist hung just outside the open doorway and grey droplets dripped from the lintel.

It's been the better part of a moon, I guess, the man said. Ever since the rainy season was supposed to end and didn't. Something's just not right. I just feel so . . . heavy.

Mm, murmured the healer. Where in the body do you feel this heaviness?

I can't really say, exactly. It's kind of everywhere. I used to jump out of bed every morning and get right to work. Now I have to force myself to get up, and I get so tired during the day. I don't feel like eating most of the time either. Food just doesn't have much taste anymore.

Mm. Any changes to your bowel movements?

I don't think so. No, not really.

How are things with the bird?

The man made a face. Nothing going on down there, he said. I just can't—you know—get in the mood. Someone must have put a curse on me and now a bad spirit's hanging around. Have you got something that can help with that? My neighbour says you gave him a poultice for the rash on his belly that cleared it right up.

A poultice won't help you any, the healer said. I've got something else for your condition. Something new I've been trying out.

The healer whistled softly. From the back of the hut a recumbent form stirred, rose, yawned, stretched, and came padding into the light.

This is my new helper, said the healer.

A dog, the man said.

Yes. Take her home with you.

And eat her?

No. Don't eat her. She'll be no use at all if you do that. Think of her like the medicine I gave your neighbour. Keep her close to you. Hug her. Pet her. Let her sleep with you.

That's it?

That's it.

And she'll draw out the bad spirit, right?

Something like that.

Right. That's why I shouldn't eat her.

Exactly. The cure only works if she stays alive and whole. Hold out your arms.

The man held out his arms. Wolf came to him and nestled against his chest.

Oh, the man said. She's warm.

He folded his arms around the dog.

How does that feel? the healer asked.

Not bad, I guess, the man said, and he smiled. It feels pretty good, actually. I think it's already working.

Good.

The man climbed to his feet. Wolf stood beside him.

I won't be able to pay you until the harvest, he told the healer.

You don't need to pay me. Pay her. She accepts fish, corn cakes, bones. Pretty much anything you've got. Keep her for a week and then come see me again.

I will. Thank you.

You're welcome. And remember, don't eat her.

Bones

The lady of the castle went smiling around the table, pouring a libation of welcome into the goblet of each guest. Her husband, the lord of the castle and the adjacent forests and fens, raised his own in a beringed hand. The neighbouring chieftain, a bitter enemy now become an ally, raised his in turn. His men followed suit.

To the new-found friendship between our houses, the lady said. Long may it endure.

Everyone else at the table, guests and vassals of the host, hoisted their own goblets, echoed the words with gusto, and quaffed deeply. A husky cheer went up to the smoke-blackened rafters.

Wolf watched from his spot behind the lord's chair, the special place he'd been awarded as first and foremost among the lord's hunting hounds. From a puppy he had been raised to give chase and take down prey, and he was the best. He knew it and knew that he had earned the spoils that came with rank. And there were so many good smells roiling in from the kitchens this

evening. The air was practically dripping with the savours of roast venison, fowl, blood pudding, mince pies. But as always, there had to be a lot of talking before any eating was done, and so the first course hadn't been brought out yet.

Wolf knew better than to utter a sound or in any way show his impatience. The lord was as taut and tense as a bowstring. This was clearly an important dinner. If Wolf put one whisker out of place, the back of a hand across his snout would be all he could expect from the evening.

The lady returned to her place beside the lord and laid a hand gently on his forearm. It was time.

The minstrels on their dais started up a spritely tune and the servers marched in bearing trenchers heaped with meat. Wolf's nose quivered and he licked his lips as hosts, retainers, and guests tucked in.

The diners barely exchanged a word as they fell to the vital business of stuffing their bellies. The devouring was long and ferocious. Plates were swiftly emptied and wiped clean of gravy with hunks of bread. More steaming courses were brought in, to the glad notes of lyre, flute, and drum. The table was thumped again and again in appreciation of the fine fare. Gobbets of flesh flew off forks and goblets were spilled. There were cries for more drink and servers hurried in with brimming flagons. Wolf couldn't help but notice that the cups of the former enemies were refilled more often than those of the host and his men. He'd seen that before and knew what was coming. This only added a further edge to his waiting.

At last the lord sat back, uttered a decisive belch—a fleeting wince wrinkled his lady's sedate brow—and tossed half of a mostly stripped roe shank behind him.

Wolf snatched the prize out of the air. Morsel firmly between his teeth, he inched himself under the master's seat, out of the path of the attendants and with his back to the greedy stares of his fellow hounds, who knew better than to challenge the favourite's right to the first spoils. He could feel their envy like heat on his back. How they all wished they were where he was. One day, one of them might just be elevated to top dog. As he had been when his predecessor was gored to death by a boar. Where would he be then?

It wasn't worth another thought. He had a far more pressing matter to attend to.

There was nothing finer, he was certain, than a bone. The first bite of cold, lifeless mineral giving way to a tapestry of contrasts—the initial hard, slippery surface yielding up a satisfying scrape and crunch as your teeth grind away and sink in, slowly breaking through to the succulent marrow nestled inside. The scent filling your nostrils a heady mix of blood-tanged relish and the smells of the hunt—horse shit and wet fur and deer musk and hound slobber, with faint mushroomy notes of the forest floor. As you work it over in your jaws the bone gets warmer and tiny bits flake off, adding a gritty feel to the palate. A riot of flavours dances over the tongue, a delightful motley of the outer layer's greasy smokiness, with traces of the cook's judicious seasoning of pepper, rosemary, basil, and thyme still providing a hint of piquancy, until at last there's a soul-satisfying crack and the marrow's warm, buttery pith is set free at last.

Wolf gnawed away and felt the old familiar desire tensing his limbs. This treasure was not meant to be polished off in one go but hidden, buried, saved for leaner times. He glanced around, looking for hiding places and finding nothing but hard flagstones and the shod feet of humans. Once the feasting was over there was a chance—a slim chance—he might abscond unnoticed with the remains of his prize and scrape a quick hole in the yard. He would have to wait and see. The harsh schooling he'd endured on how to leash his impulses until given the go-ahead had its benefits. These inhibitions had been bred into him too, as the scion of a long line of hunters and trackers who

had accompanied their masters on the chase. He—they—didn't pursue and take down prey for food as hounds of lesser breeds did—the lord's pens were plentifully stocked with hogs and sheep. They hunted simply because it was *the hunt*, the immemorial pastime of those born to rule. Striding the forests and battlefields of World, picking out and slaughtering the weakest in any herd, four-footed or two-footed.

To disobey your lord and master made you not simply a bad dog. It made you a turncoat, a betrayer. Breaker of an oath pledged by your ancestors with their blood, long before you were born.

The lady touched her lord's arm once more. It was time for her to retire for the evening. From this point, as Wolf well knew, the festivities would take a turn that she preferred not to see. She rose and the lord kissed her hand. The visiting chieftain rose and bowed to her and she tilted her head his way, then took her leave, gliding gracefully across the rush-strewn flagstones and up the stairs to her chamber, where maids were waiting to attend her. Moments later Wolf's ears caught the faint music of harp and soft voices lilting in unison, sweet sounds that would help the lady ignore the coming uproar.

The lord spat a chunk of gristle onto his plate, wiped his mouth on his sleeve, and rose from his seat. He was about to speak more words.

Always more words.

There was a time, the lord said, raising a hand for quiet. There was a time when we would never let the sun go down on an insult or an affront without marching out with sword in hand to take vengeance.

The lord, it occurred to Wolf, had bones inside of him. All humans did. He had seen them hanging from gibbets. He'd dug such bones out of shallow pits not far from the castle. He'd glimpsed them lying under the water at the bottom of the castle's weedy moat, being kissed by inquisitive little fish.

He had bones inside him too.

Those dark days, the lord went on, are thankfully behind us.

Hear, hear, a fat old retainer shouted.

Wolf had heard variations on this speech many times before. It meant dessert wasn't far off.

Now, the lord said, when insult is given, we have other, less crude methods to make things right. We can come together like this and find a better way to redress the wrongs that have been done. A more . . . civilized way.

The visiting chieftain had risen unsteadily, assuming this was a prelude to yet another toast. He'd downed a great deal of drink along with his dinner and now he looked at the goblet in his hand as if puzzled by how it had gotten there. Then he glanced up at the lord and finally seemed to sense the icy current beneath the fine phrases. Dim understanding grew in his face. He turned to his retainers and mumbled something inaudible, his words oozing thickly like the sludge of the moat in which Wolf had sunk his paws once to get at those drowned bones. The chieftain's retainers scrambled for their daggers, but they were too slow. Far too slow. The particular tincture added by the lady of the castle to their drink—and picked up by Wolf's keen nose—had made sure of that.

The castle guards rushed in with blades drawn and the slaughter commenced. There were curses and hoarse cries, the ring of metal, shrieks and groans, the thud of bodies hitting the floor. In the chaos the table got upset and stray crusts and scraps were scattered across the bloodstained flagstones. Wolf ignored them. He sat by the lord's chair, watching the guests fall one by one. On several occasions in the past he'd been asked to bring down this sort of prey, but never in the banqueting hall. In the hall he and the other dogs had learned from brutal correction not to move a muscle unless bidden, so that hounds and men would not get in one another's way.

At last the tumult and stabbing was over. A breathy quiet fell. Upstairs, the harp and the sweet voices flowed on in tranquil

measure. The lord hadn't moved from where he'd been standing, and now he sat back down. As master, it was his privilege to observe without getting his robes dirty. He gave a low grunt of satisfaction, reached behind his chair, and scratched Wolf between the ears.

Wolf noticed that the lord's fleshy fingers, with all the little bones tucked inside, were trembling just a little. He felt something odd within, a small, cold stab, as if a tiny sliver of bone from his meal had broken off and found its way to his heart.

What did it mean?

A dark rivulet came trickling along the seams between the flagstones. It slid lazily past Wolf. He stretched his neck and took one cautious lick. Then another. The familiar taste soothed his agitation. It would be all right. He understood that all punishments had been meted out for the evening and that by remaining quiet he had done his part to make sure the proceedings went as planned. The lord would retire soon to his own chamber, another successful negotiation concluded, taking his favourite hound with him to help keep the dark at bay.

Banana

A young monk came to the old monk and asked, Master, does a dog have Buddha Nature or not?

No, the old monk answered.

The next day the young monk returned to the old monk's hut.

Dear Master, he said, according to the Enlightened One's teachings, all beings have Buddha Nature. Which means, if I understand right, all beings have the potential to awaken from delusion to the truth of existence. But you say that a dog does not. I think that what you were really trying to tell me is that the phenomenon we call a dog cannot be separated from anything else in the universe. Because the true nature of existence is that everything is one. Which means there really is no such thing as *dog*. It's a label, not reality. That's why the answer to the question is *no*, right?

The old monk answered, No.

———

The monk waited three days, until he couldn't stand it any longer. He went to see the master again.

Master, he said, when I came to this monastery six years ago I was driven by a sincere desire to cast off all worldly attachments and find enlightenment. I knew that the road would be hard. I didn't kid myself about that. But I've come to a wall that has no door, and I feel even more lost and confused than when I started. If human beings have the seed of a Buddha within them, then a dog must have it too. We're made of the same stuff, after all. A dog may not be able to speak, but surely it has a mind and it thinks and feels in its own way, doesn't it? So please, Master, I'm begging you, please explain to me why a dog doesn't have Buddha Nature, or I'll have to hand in my robe and leave the monastery.

The old monk sighed and said, Well, let's see. Whose dog are we talking about here?

Forgive me, Master, I meant any dog. You know, just dogs in general.

I don't know any dogs of that kind. You had better go find a dog and bring it here so we can be sure we're referring to the same dog.

Go . . . find a dog?

Yes. Find a dog and bring it here. And we'll investigate.

The monk shook his head as he walked away.

Find a dog. Right. Okay.

Wolf was living on the street in those days, having had enough of masters and their incessant demands. In fact, she had pretty much given up speaking with humans. Back when all they did was hunt and barely survive she could understand them and they could understand her, or at least enough to get by. But nowadays the humans had—and did—so many strange new things. Planting and harvesting the grains they liked rather than just picking them where they happened to grow. Fencing in the prey instead of wandering around looking for them. Living in crowded cities and inventing all these noisy machines, things that Wolf couldn't see the point of.

I've stayed *me*, she often thought, but they've changed.

Wolf herself hung out a lot in front of a fishmonger's shop. Other merchants usually yelled at her and chased her away with brooms, but the fishmonger would sometimes throw her a few tasty scraps.

Which is why the young monk found her sitting in front of the fishmonger's.

Is this your dog? he asked the fishmonger, a notoriously cranky old woman with one blind eye.

No, the fishmonger said. Not mine. Not anybody's.

The monk returned that afternoon to the old monk's hut with Wolf leashed on a length of rope. The old monk was deep in meditation. The monk untied the dog at the door and she entered this unfamiliar space cautiously, sniffing along the walls and in every corner. When she'd satisfied herself there was no danger and nothing to eat, she sat in front of the old monk to see what would happen next. This old human was completely at ease and therefore quite obviously the top dog around this place.

Master, here's a dog, the monk said softly.

The old monk stirred.

A dog?

Yes, Master. You asked me to go find a dog. This is the one I found.

This is the dog you were talking about yesterday?

Well, no. Not exactly. Not this particular dog. It was the first one I could find on short notice.

She's pretty. If it is a she.

I think so, Master, yes. I found it in town, hanging around the fishmonger's shop. It's a stray.

A stray what?

Dog, Master. A stray dog.

A stray dog? Where?

This one, Master. The dog you're petting right now.

But this dog is sitting here with me. She's not straying anywhere.

No, not at the moment, but—

Dear novice, I think you had better leave the dog with me. I will need to ponder these questions further.

Yes, Master. Thank you, Master.

Oh, and please set aside some rice and fish from my dinner this evening. And bring a bowl of milk, too. This animal looks very thin and undernourished.

The next day the young monk came to see the master and found him playing with the dog.

Master, he said, I was wondering if perhaps you'd come to an answer yet.

About what?

About whether dogs have, you know . . .

Fleas? The old monk regarded Wolf critically. Do you think so? She is quite the mess, it's true. Her paws are filthy and her fur is badly matted. She could really use a bath and a good brushing.

I will bring some soap and water, Master.

Thank you, dear novice. By the way, I've consulted the *Book of Beasts*. It says there are three types of dogs: hunting, guarding, and edible. Which would you say she is?

Well . . . none of them, Master.

I agree. Another puzzle we will have to solve.

When the young monk visited the master the following day, the old monk was brushing Wolf's fur.

The dog's coat looks much better now, Master.

Yes, the master said, beaming, and I have an answer to your question.
You do?
You wondered if she had fleas. She doesn't.
Oh. That's good.

When the young monk came to bring the master his midday meal, he found the old monk sitting watching the dog sleep. The young monk set down the plate and went away without saying anything. He thought it best not to disturb them.

The young monk came to see the master the next morning. To his surprise—tinged with some guilty relief—the dog wasn't there.
Master, where is . . . ?
Oh, Banana is out in the garden, sniffing around.
Banana?
I named her Banana. I love bananas. Do you like bananas?
Sure, the monk said with a shrug. I like them okay.
Banana has learned her own name already, the old monk said.
Has she?
Banana! the old monk called. Here, girl!
After a moment Wolf came padding in and went straight to the master, who fed her a rice ball.
What do you say, Banana, do you like your name?
WOOF, Wolf said.

The young monk hurried to see the master.
Dear Master, he said, I had the most incredible experience last night. I was meditating as usual in my cell before going to bed and suddenly I wasn't there. I wasn't anywhere. There was just . . . peace. It was like everything was a calm pool of silky white milk. I think it might have been satori, Master. I think I glimpsed it. Just for a moment.

That's nice, the old monk said. Can you help me with Banana? She's been throwing up. I think she ate something she shouldn't have.

The old master gave the young monk a new practice to help calm his restless heart. He was to walk around the entire monastery grounds twice every day, once in the morning and once in the evening, reciting the Heart Sutra. And he was to take Banana with him on these walks and recite the sutra to her.

She could use the exercise anyhow, the old monk said.

The young monk dutifully walked the dog around the monastery grounds every day, first thing in the morning and in the evening, reciting the Heart Sutra.

All things are in themselves neither good nor bad, the monk recited as he walked. *Everything is empty of self-existence. Things do not appear or disappear, they are not tainted nor pure, they do not increase or decrease. In this luminous emptiness there are no forms, no feelings, no perceptions, no impulses. No eyes, no ears, no nose, no tongue, no body, no mind. No colour, no sound, no smell, no taste, no touch, no objects of mind. No ignorance and no end to ignorance, no old age or death, no suffering. No enlightenment, nothing to seek, and nothing to attain.*

Wolf would stop from time to time to pee, sniff among the pathside grasses, or prick up her ears at the sound of a squirrel in the trees.

What do you make of that, dog? the monk asked. No nose—that means no smells. No eyes, ears, tongue . . . No squirrels, either. It's all emptiness. *Mu.* Whatever that is. I thought I knew, but I realize I was just kidding myself. I honestly don't have a clue anymore. What do you think?

Wolf looked up at the monk, tongue out, panting happily.

Great, the monk said. Now I'm talking to you.

During afternoon meditation the young monk fell asleep on his cushion and dreamed that Wolf was dressed in a monk's robe and sitting in the master's chair. A soft glow came off the dog's fur, suffusing the room with warmth and peace.

The master brought the young monk over to see this. He praised the dog's ability to sit still for such a long period of time.

She's the finest pupil I've ever taught, the master said. She's sure to become a Bodhisattva long before any of you slackers.

The young monk woke abruptly from the dream, his teeth hurting from having ground them so hard in his sleep.

What am I doing here? he asked himself. That old monk is the absolute cliché of the inscrutable Zen master, tossing out riddles and pointless fables, and I lap it up and come crawling back for more, desperate for the magic words that will turn me into a Buddha just like that, one, two, three, *poof.* What a farce. What a racket. I've been such a fool, wasting my life on this meaningless nonsense. And meanwhile my master pays far more attention to that mangy animal than he does to me. And the useless mutt just basks in it. *Dear novice* my ass. Damn that animal. Enough is enough. I'm marching over to the master's hut right now and handing in my resignation.

The monk came to see the master and found him cleaning up a foul puddle of liquid shit in the corner of the hut.

Oh, Master, no. Let me take care of that for you.

Thank you, dear novice. I don't know what's gotten into Banana today. Or what's coming out of her, I should say.

It doesn't look good, Master. And oh, that smell.

The monk returned later and found the old monk kneeling beside Wolf, who was lying on the floor of the hut, panting.

Is she worse, Master?

The old monk answered, I think she's really sick. She hasn't moved from this spot or eaten anything all morning.

I'm sorry, Master. What can I do?

You wouldn't happen to know anything about canine disorders?

I'm afraid not, Master. We could try taking her to the apothecary. He treats people's pets sometimes, I've heard. He might know what to do.

Yes, that's a good idea. How long has Banana been with us at the monastery, would you say?

Well, it's been about a month, Master. The magnolias hadn't yet budded when I found her, and now they're in full bloom.

They are. How beautiful. How wonderful that the flowers bloom first, before the leaves come out.

I will take Banana to the apothecary, Master.

Thank you, dear novice. I knew I could count on you.

The monk returned to the master without the dog.

Where is Banana?

She's fine, Master. Or she will be. The apothecary fed her some herbs and is keeping her overnight, just to be on the safe side. If things go well, I'll be able to pick her up tomorrow.

Oh, I'm so glad to hear that. This business of dogs is more complicated than we thought. Don't you agree?

I do, Master.

We'll just have to keep at it until we reach some kind of an answer.

We will, Master.

The young monk sat in the reception area of the apothecary's shop, waiting for Wolf to be brought out to him.

The only other person there was a woman with a small cat lying asleep in her lap.

Dog or cat? the woman asked the young monk.

I'm sorry?

Do you have a dog or a cat here?

Oh, a dog. I mean, it's not my dog. It's someone else's. I'm just picking her up.

I like dogs, but they make my husband sneeze his head off. Not cats, though. Thank goodness for that. We just love animals.

When I was a kid my father wouldn't let us have a dog. He didn't like dogs. It's what he used to say: *I don't like dogs.*

Really? Do you know why?

Well, I've never been sure. But he worked in a slaughtering yard all his life. He killed pigs for a living, but I'm sure he never really loved what he did. In later years it started to get to him, I think. The killing itself, the ending of a life, even an animal's life, really started to bother him. I'm sure of it. He had to detach himself from what he was doing. I could see the change in his eyes when he got ready to go to work. I could see it happen. It was like—I don't know—like he was hiding his own face in wrapping paper. And I think that's why he said no to us, to my brother and my sisters and me, when we bugged him and my mom to let us get a dog. And we bugged them a lot.

The monk laughed.

But in the end, I think he had to keep the animals *out there.* Separate, you know? He didn't like dogs because they reminded him of what he did for a living. Killing things.

Maybe he didn't really dislike dogs. Maybe it was just the opposite.

The opposite?

Yes. What he felt deep down wasn't dislike at all.

The opposite. That's it. Why did I never think of that? Yes, you're right, that's why he couldn't have a dog in the house.

The monk stared at the far wall of the room without seeing it. He saw the master waiting for him in his hut. He saw his father going out the door to work. He saw a bowl of milk. He saw a field of grass bowing in the wind.

The monk smiled and murmured to himself, Go find a dog.

Pardon? the woman asked.

Oh, sorry, just something my master said.

If you don't mind me asking, how did you become a . . .

A monk? It came out of nowhere. I was an apprentice pottery painter. I was sitting at the door of the shop working one day when a monk walked by, ringing his bell. I hadn't paid them any attention before. That world seemed beyond me. The monk didn't say a word, just gave me a glance, and all of a sudden I *knew*. I had to become like him. My parents never really approved of my career change, but they didn't stand in the way. I think it hurt my father to see me leave, though. The day I left home to come to the monastery he had the same look on his face I saw on him when he was going off to work. Just before I walked out the door he asked me—

The apothecary appeared with Wolf on a leash.

Here she is, said the apothecary.

Oh, the monk said, there you are.

Wolf's tail whipped back and forth. She hadn't been sure she would see this particular human again, and she knew now that she'd wanted to, and the old one as well. If humans could be like this, there was something to be said for staying with them. At least for a while.

She's beautiful, the woman said.

Wolf jumped up into the monk's arms and licked his face.

What a good girl, Banana, he said, his voice breaking. You're such a good girl.

She's going to be fine, the apothecary said. I've put together a mixture for her to take over the next few days. Other than that, let her rest and make sure she has plenty of water.

Thank you. Yes, I will. Thank you.

The apothecary bowed and walked away.

Well, it was nice meeting you, the woman said to the young monk.

You too. I hope your cat will be all right.

We're having her put down, actually. I am, I mean. My husband's waiting outside. He just couldn't face being there when . . . you know.

Oh. I'm sorry.

Well, she's old now and can't really walk anymore, and she's in a lot of pain. So, you know, it seems the kindest thing to do.

It's not easy, is it.

It isn't. But didn't the Buddha say we shouldn't get attached to things?

The monk scratched Wolf behind the ears, then he laughed.

Right. He did say that. What do you think, Banana? Should we get attached to things or not?

Wolf licked the monk's face.

No, we shouldn't, should we, the monk said. No.

Beast

MAGISTRATE: Hound known as Wolf, belonging to Jehanne Dufay, widow of Dufay the ropemaker, you have been brought before this court to answer a most serious charge. It is alleged that on Lady Day in this year of our Lord fourteen hundred and sixty-seven, at half past three of the town clock, you did flee your mistress's keeping to run wild in the streets, whereupon you did leap over a wall and wantonly murder seven laying hens and a prize cock belonging to Godbert de Lauge, the stonemason, and what is more, you did savagely attack the stonemason and inflict grievous injuries upon him, including the shredding of a new woolen tunic, a bite on the . . . *hmm* . . . fundament, and the loss of a finger.

WOLF: Hello! I need to pee.

MAGISTRATE: Court clerk, have it entered into the record that the hound named Wolf just growled menacingly at this bench. Advocate for the accused, restrain your client.

ADVOCATE BARTHÉLEMY: That was not a growl, Your Honour. It was more of an excited whine. As you can see, my client is wagging his tail in a most amiable manner.

WOLF: This is boring. Come on, let's play!

MAGISTRATE: Clerk, have it entered into the record that the hound Wolf did just bark threateningly at this bench.

ADVOCATE BARTHÉLEMY: Surely not, Your Honour. That was but a merry woof.

MAGISTRATE: Advocate for the accused, we advise you to stop contradicting us.

ADVOCATE BARTHÉLEMY: Yes, Your Honour.

MAGISTRATE: This letter informs me, Maître Barthélemy, that you were sent from Paris, having made a name for yourself representing brute beasts in cases of law.

ADVOCATE BARTHÉLEMY: I was, Your Honour. I have.

MAGISTRATE: It says here that you defended a donkey accused of trampling a child to death. And further, you argued on behalf of a swarm of bees accused of stinging some pious old women on their way to Mass in d'Ambrac. One of these good women, so it says, swelled up like a gourd and died. I am curious, Advocate, what verdicts were rendered in these cases.

ADVOCATE BARTHÉLEMY: The donkey was regrettably found guilty and flayed, Your Honour, despite my best efforts. The bees were pardoned with a reprimand, as I proved that the old woman who unfortunately passed away had but one sting on

her body, which meant that the entire swarm could not be held responsible. In that case there were certain precedents in law which I was able to—

MAGISTRATE: Thank you, Advocate, that will do. In this case before us, what does your client have to say to the charges we have read? Or what have you to say for him?

ADVOCATE BARTHÉLEMY: My client is not guilty, Your Honour, as I shall prove to this court. Indeed, as I hope to demonstrate, the very idea that a hound—

GODBERT DE LAUGE: There's no need for any more of this palaver, Your Honour. The hound did it and I have the scars to prove it's so. Oh, he was named right, that one, by the Holy Martyr he was. Wolf he is and wolf he does. Look at him curl his lip at me. He's just itching to finish what he started.

WOLF: You hurt me. You're a bad human.

MAGISTRATE: Do not tell us *that* was not a growl, Advocate.

ADVOCATE BARTHÉLEMY: I will concede it may have been, Your Honour. (To Wolf) *Easy.*

GODBERT DE LAUGE: You see, Your Honour? Showing himself for what he really is. Just as he did when I found him with my good Chanticleer in his jaws, shaking him, and the blood spraying everywhere like Sainte Geneviève's fountain, and all my lovely plump white hens lying dead in the dirt, those fine stout egg-layers, and ah, the coin they bring in. All of it gone just like that. By heaven, I would've come out sooner to stop him, but I was speaking with good Friar Bouvarde at my door and I didn't hear the commotion until it was too late.

ADVOCATE BARTHÉLEMY: The friar informed me that he found you passed out drunk in your doorway and was compelled to rouse you.

GODBERT DE LAUGE: By Christ, if the friar said that, he's lying, damn his pox-ridden soul to hell.

MAGISTRATE: Curb your tongue, stonemason, or you will be removed from this court. And, Advocate for the accused, we caution you to refrain from hearsay. Stonemason, resume your account.

GODBERT DE LAUGE: Thank you, Your Honour. So that accursed hound had my Chanticleer in his jaws, as I've said, and I ran to free him and that's when the demon set upon me and tore my new tunic, and then, when I tried to get away, he sank his teeth into my arse. But he wasn't done with me then, oh no. When I raised my hand to defend myself he bit off my finger. See, here. The pointing finger on my left hand. Gone. Bitten clean off. The hand with which I earn my bread, Your Honour. I'm a cripple now, Your Honour, and it's all thanks to that hell beast there, laughing in his devil's heart.

ADVOCATE BARTHÉLEMY: That wound looks remarkably healed, stonemason, for such a recent injury. I submit that you cut off your own finger some time ago, perhaps while plying your trade under the influence of strong wine.

GODBERT DE LAUGE: You lie, you pointy-headed little bookworm. I'd give good coin you've never been inside a woman's cunny in your life.

ADVOCATE BARTHÉLEMY: I was given birth to, like all men, stonemason, so you would lose that wager.

GODBERT DE LAUGE: You . . . you *lawyer*, I'll beat you within an inch of your worthless life.

ADVOCATE BARTHÉLEMY: As you did the hound?

GODBERT DE LAUGE: Worse. No, I mean . . . He's lying, Your Honour. He's tricked me, the pasty little cockroach. I never laid a finger on the hound before it went for me.

MAGISTRATE: Silence, both of you! A farce will not be made of these proceedings or I promise you there will be necks in stocks. Do I make myself clear?

ADVOCATE BARTHÉLEMY: Absolutely, Your Honour.

GODBERT DE LAUGE: Begging your pardon, Your Honour. But see these wounds. The truth is plain as day. And what if the beast has the *rage*? God protect me, what if I start foaming at the mouth and running mad?

MAGISTRATE: I must say it wouldn't surprise me, stonemason.

ADVOCATE BARTHÉLEMY: Your Honour, it's quite obvious the hound is not afflicted with that malady.

MAGISTRATE: That remains to be determined. Let us speak with the dog's master. (Reading a paper.) Or mistress, as the case appears to be. The court calls the Widow Dufay to the stand.

BAILIFF: The Widow Dufay to the stand! The Widow Dufay!

JEHANNE DUFAY: Here I am, Your Honour. No need for your lackey to deafen me.

MAGISTRATE: Is this your hound, good woman?

JEHANNE DUFAY: It is, Your Honour. My good hound Wolf.

MAGISTRATE: Then tell us, does this animal have the rage that can be passed to Man through a bite? In short, is this a mad dog?

JEHANNE DUFAY: If he had the rage, Your Honour, he'd be biting someone right now.

MAGISTRATE: Yes. Well. That seems reasonable. Let us carry on. Good woman, pray tell the court what you were doing on Lady Day last, at or about three of the town clock.

JEHANNE DUFAY: Chasing after my youngest, Your Honour, as usual. My little Remy. He'd dashed out the gate without a stitch on, as he often does. Oh, he's a wild one, Your Honour. Not more than two and loves to gambol about in his birthday suit and chase after birds and rabbits. He'll be off for a soldier before he can talk, that one.

MAGISTRATE: Yes, yes, and where was your hound, the aforementioned Wolf, while you were retrieving your errant offspring?

JEHANNE DUFAY: Ah, Your Honour, in my haste and worry I left the yard gate ajar, and my Wolf, he must have slipped out when I wasn't looking. I do my best to keep him at home, truly I do, but he's much like my Remy. He loves to wander when he spies his chance.

MAGISTRATE: Do you mean to say that you, the widow of a ropemaker, have not sufficient of your husband's stock left to tie up a hound?

JEHANNE DUFAY: Oh, I never tie him, Your Honour. He's a friendly sort, as harmless and loving as a dove. With decent Christian folk, leastways. Aren't you, my good Wolf?

WOLF (eagerly): I love you! Can we go home now?

MAGISTRATE: Advocate for the accused, we advise you to restrain your client from any more of these outbursts. Whimpering and whining will not be tolerated before this bench.

ADVOCATE BARTHÉLEMY: Of course, Your Honour. (To Wolf) *I warned you.*

MAGISTRATE: Proceed, good woman.

JEHANNE DUFAY: You can ask anyone in the town. They all know my Wolf. I found him on my doorstep one morning, just a little poppet he was, looking so ill-used and hungry I had not the heart to drive him away. I took him in and fed him, and he has repaid me that small kindness many times over, minding my children and chasing off men who think to bully me into wedlock, or at least into bed. At first I did tie Wolf in the yard of nights, but he howled so piteously I let him sleep indoors, by the hearth. He hasn't much for wits, it's true, but he's never been any trouble to anyone that I know of. Yes, he's slipped out of the yard before, I can't deny it. But he greets every soul good-naturedly, and our townsfolk are happy to see him and they feed him tidbits from their hands. He barks and growls at de Lauge because that wicked old tosspot kicked him in the street.

GODBERT DE LAUGE: I did not. How the whore slanders me, Your Honour. I'd stake my last farthing she's a witch and the hound is her demon lackey. We all know witches like to keep cats and dogs around. They say she hexed her man and gave him the lump on his neck that sent him to his grave.

JEHANNE DUFAY: Who says so? Only you, you shameless liar. If my Gilles—God rest him—was here, you wouldn't dare open your mouth, you coward.

MAGISTRATE: *Enough*, both of you.

JEHANNE DUFAY: My Wolf's a trueborn hound, Your Honour. And hounds will roam. That's the urging God put into their hearts, to wander as they may and seek what pleases them. A hound doesn't like a rope around his neck any more than does a man. And why would that be so if the good Lord didn't wish it to be so? Yes, they stay by us, out of the love that can grow between our kind and theirs, but at bottom the good Lord made them wandering souls, and that's the truth of it. One time he strayed I found him in the marketplace. I watched him greet the stonemason de Lauge without fear and the stonemason returned his trust with a boot to the ribs. Then what did my Wolf do, in the innocence of his loving heart? He came right back to de Lauge and licked his dirty hand. Yes, he did. My Wolf licked his hand. And what did he get for it? Another kick, this time to the muzzle, which sent him sprawling and knocked out two of his teeth. For days after he wasn't right in the head, poor thing. My Wolf turned the other cheek, Your Honour, as our Saviour bade us do, and that's what it got him.

MAGISTRATE: This dumb brute's knowledge of our Lord's gospels hardly matters in the present case. What say you, Widow Dufay, to the accusation that your hound murdered the fowl belonging to the stonemason and inflicted these wounds upon him?

JEHANNE DUFAY: In truth he's chased and killed rabbits before. And pheasants. If it runs he'll chase it and bring it down, if he can. He might kill a hen, to be sure. I can't deny it. You might say Nature put that desire in his heart as well.

MAGISTRATE: Nature is not at issue here, my good woman. Crime, and public safety, are what concern us. Is there anyone else who will come forward at this time to corroborate or refute the charges that have been laid against the widow's hound? We call for further witnesses.

BAILIFF: Further witnesses! Any further witnesses! Come forward!

BUTCHER'S ROBIN (raising his voice): I saw the hound that day.

MAGISTRATE: Step forward, boy. Your name?

BUTCHER'S ROBIN: My father named me Amal, Your Majesty, but everyone calls me Robin because I love to sing. I was apprenticed last year to Fat Floquet, the butcher.

WOLF: Hello! You're fun! Want to play?

MAGISTRATE: Advocate for the accused, another outburst from your client and you will be found in contempt. And lad, *Your Honour* will do. Tell us what you saw, and remember that before God and this assembly you must speak the truth and nothing but the truth.

BUTCHER'S ROBIN: May God strike me down if I don't, Your Honour. This is how it was. I was coming along the lane by the stonemason's yard with my wheelbarrow, singing a ditty that

Perroquin the minstrel taught me. He's hunchbacked and a dwarf, and folk tease him for it and cuff him about, but oh, he has the voice of an angel—

ADVOCATE BARTHÉLEMY: May I ask what you were doing with the wheelbarrow, my boy?

BUTCHER'S ROBIN: Carting guts to the town ashpit, monsieur.

ADVOCATE BARTHÉLEMY: What sort of guts?

BUTCHER'S ROBIN: Pigs' guts, monsieur. As I do every day but the Lord's.

ADVOCATE BARTHÉLEMY: So the wheelbarrow held a load of pigs' guts.

BUTCHER'S ROBIN: What else? My master, Floquet, he'd just done for a pair of the mayor's fattest hogs and told me to haul the guts to the pit.

ADVOCATE BARTHÉLEMY: This load of offal must have produced quite the smell.

BUTCHER'S ROBIN: Oh, it stank to Saint Peter's nose, monsieur. It always does.

MAGISTRATE: And that is when you saw the hound, boy? The one before you now?

BUTCHER'S ROBIN: I did, Your Honour, and that's him all right. Good old Wolf. He came leaping over the stonemason's wall, at the place where it's fallen down and Monsieur de Lauge hasn't

repaired it yet. Wolf nearly barrelled into me, he was running so mad, and I heard the stonemason howling and cursing, using words I was taught not to repeat to my betters.

ADVOCATE BARTHÉLEMY: You were previously acquainted with this hound?

BUTCHER'S ROBIN: Sorry, monsieur, was I what?

ADVOCATE BARTHÉLEMY: You know this hound?

BUTCHER'S ROBIN: Oh yes. Everyone knows Wolf. We're antiquated to be sure, as you say. I throw him odds and ends whenever I see him, and many's the time he's walked a piece of the road with me. Wolf is a merry soul, sir. He likes to sing along with me, in his own way. It cheers my heart to hear him yowling.

ADVOCATE BARTHÉLEMY: I'm sure it does. What I'd like to know—and think carefully about this, my boy—is it possible that the hound ran toward you because of the enticing odours from your wheelbarrow? Enticing to a hound, at least. More to the point, might I suggest he ran to you in expectation of some of those odds and ends that you are wont to throw him?

BUTCHER'S ROBIN: Well, I thought so at first, monsieur, but he tore right past me like the Evil One was after his soul, and his muzzle covered in blood and feathers, plain as day. And I thought, Oh no, Wolf, what trouble have you brought down on yourself, my friend? He'd done something he shouldn't have, sure enough.

ADVOCATE BARTHÉLEMY: But you couldn't be certain of what he had done or not done, could you. What you figured or imagined is not what you actually saw.

BUTCHER'S ROBIN: Oh, I never imagine anything, monsieur. Not me. That's what my master, Floquet, tells me. He says I have a block of wood for a head and can't make up a story to save my life. No, it was clear what Wolf had done. It was wrong of him to kill those birds and bite Monsieur de Lauge, I suppose, but he's a good sort, Your Honour. *He* didn't think it was wrong, you may be sure, and I hope it won't go hard for him.

MAGISTRATE: It is not your place to plead for the animal, butcher's boy. You say you heard the stonemason cursing and howling in his yard. Did you see him?

BUTCHER'S ROBIN: I didn't, Your Honour, as there was a wall between me and him. But I heard him all right.

MAGISTRATE: And hearing these cries, did it not occur to you, as a good Christian, to go to his aid?

BUTCHER'S ROBIN: Forgive me, but it didn't, Your Honour. I've heard Monsieur de Lauge in his yard many times, roaring and swinging that cudgel of his like he was bent on caving skulls in. And at that same hour, mostly, which is when he's like to get into the wine and curse his bad luck. And women. And the King. We've all heard his carrying on, Your Honour, and we know better than to go near him when he's in that humour. Poor Wolf picked the worst time to set upon those hens.

GODBERT DE LAUGE: I've never said a word against the King, you blackamoor. You Egyptian. More lies, Your Honour. First the witch and now this halfwit. The folk of this town have it in for me, Your Honour. They hate me. They've persecuted and slandered me without end, all because my poor sainted father was a tax collector.

JEHANNE DUFAY: He was hanged as a thief in Girouxville.

GODBERT DE LAUGE: On the word of a Jew.

MAGISTRATE (firmly): What have we said about these disruptions? Butcher's boy, you may step down. Advocate for the accused, we must say the evidence we've heard tells eloquently against your client. However, since you have the right to make a final summation, you may proceed. And pray endeavour to be brief. The mention of swine has reminded us it is getting on to dinnertime and there are yet more cases to be heard.

ADVOCATE BARTHÉLEMY: Thank you, Your Honour. I will be epigrammatic to a fault.

 The sage Pythagoras of mighty renown once rebuked a man who was beating a hound by saying, *That is a friend of mine you are beating, monsieur. I know him by his voice.* While Diogenes of Sinope, called the Dog for living solely by the dictates of Nature, asserted that dogs nuzzle the kind and bite only scoundrels. And from none other than the august head of Themistius the Wise of Constantinople comes a truth anyone who has kept a dog would affirm, that dogs keep watch over human beings not to ensure that they do not lose their property, but rather that they do not get robbed of their integrity. Last, we cannot forget our very own Saint Guinefort, the selfless French hound of yore, who saved a child from a wicked serpent and was wrongly slain by his master, and for this selfless act did he justly enter the august annals of faithful beasts who—

MAGISTRATE: Maître, please. This is not ancient Rome and you are not Cicero. We requested brevity.

ADVOCATE BARTHÉLEMY: I ask pardon, Your Honour. I will proceed directly to the meat of the issue, if I may say so (smiling at his own jest). I ask Robin, the butcher's boy, to come forward again and stand here, beside my client.

MAGISTRATE: You may do so, butcher's boy.

ADVOCATE BARTHÉLEMY: That's it, lad. Stand right here. Good.

WOLF (jumping up on Butcher's Robin): Hello! You smell of pig! Let's sing!

BUTCHER'S ROBIN (crouching and nuzzling Wolf): Hey, boy. You're a fine fellow. You just let them all know what a fine fellow you are and this chain will be off quick as a wink.

MAGISTRATE: Advocate for the accused, this is a travelling court, not a travelling circus. What is the purpose of this unseemly display?

ADVOCATE BARTHÉLEMY: I beg your indulgence, Your Honour—my object shall be clear in a moment. I call Godbert de Lauge the stonemason to come forward and stand at the other side of my client.

GODBERT DE LAUGE: I won't do it, Your Honour. I won't give that devil another chance to sink his fangs into my flesh.

ADVOCATE BARTHÉLEMY: Tell me, Monsieur de Lauge, why do you believe that my client would greet you any differently than he did the boy?

GODBERT DE LAUGE: The boy has the stench of the slaughter-house on him, that's why the greedy mongrel slobbered all over him just now. No, by the Holy Mother, I know what I'll get if I go near the brute again.

ADVOCATE BARTHÉLEMY: Or could it be that, as the Widow Dufay has related to us, with you having kicked this hound numerous times in the street—

GODBERT DE LAUGE: Twice only it was, by God's teeth.

ADVOCATE BARTHÉLEMY: Having kicked Wolf twice in the street, could it be that he grew afraid of you, or at the least felt a justified antipathy toward you, so that when you allegedly found him in your yard and came at him drunkenly, with cudgel on high, he feared for his life and did what all stout-hearted creatures do when threatened with mortal peril, rising to defend himself against his persecutor?

GODBERT DE LAUGE: Ha! Got you now, you puffed-up little arse-fart. I did find him in my yard, killing my fowl, just as you say. Your Honour, this prancing sodomite from *Paris* has just admitted the hound did it. You all heard him.

ADVOCATE BARTHÉLEMY: I do not deny the possibility that my client is guilty of killing the birds. If the chance arose, any hound hereabouts might have done as much. A dog is given its nature by the Creator of all, to seek what pleases it and flee what it hates, as the good Widow Dufay has rightly said. Why, the native impulse that *may* have spurred my client to go after the hens is the same one we applaud in our hunting hounds when they chase the deer and the fox at our prompting. Should we condemn on the one hand what we praise on the other? That would be illogical and hypocritical. So much, then, for the absurd charge of murdering the hens. As for the alleged attack upon the stonemason, common sense urges that any such attack, if it took place, would have been an act of self-preservation on the part of my client, as I trust I have proven beyond doubt. To conclude, Your Honour,

I submit that this hound cannot be held responsible for his actions, indeed should never have been tried in a court of law to begin with, both because he is a creature that acts solely on the promptings of his nature and because, as we have learned today, his supposed victim was in fact his tormentor.

MAGISTRATE: Do you rest your case, Advocate for the accused?

ADVOCATE BARTHÉLEMY: I do, Your Honour.

MAGISTRATE: Very well. Before we render our verdict, we call the hound named Wolf to testify in his own defence.

BAILIFF: Hound! Come forward!

MAGISTRATE: Bailiff, just take up the chain and lead him to me. There. Good. Now, hound, speak.

WOLF: . . .

MAGISTRATE: Speak, hound. Enlighten us as to what provoked your depredations.

WOLF: . . .

MAGISTRATE: Do you refuse to speak? Will you give no answer to these accusations? You forget I have the power to condemn you or show you mercy.

WOLF: . . .

MAGISTRATE: It would appear, Advocate, that your client has nothing to say in his defence.

ADVOCATE BARTHÉLEMY: With respect, Your Honour, you know as well as I that my client is incapable of the speech of men.

MAGISTRATE: We are quite aware of the fact. Just as we know that you cannot possibly divine what thoughts and urgings move this beast to act as it does. It is for no one but God to discern what likes or dislikes the hound harbours toward any man, woman, or child in this madhouse of a town I pray never to visit again. We cannot presume to trespass where only our Lord may tread. With our earthly power of reason, finite as it is, we may only judge and find fault by way of actions and consequences. And we are confident in this instance what those actions were, who the offender was that carried them out, and, most crucially, the consequences they had, namely the loss and injury incurred by Godbert de Lauge, the stonemason, at the jaws of Wolf, the hound belonging to the Widow Dufay. These facts have been established to my satisfaction. We cannot permit brute beasts free rein to bite off the fingers of honest working folk and wreak havoc as it pleases them. Therefore, it is the judgment of this court that Madame Dufay, as owner of the accused, will pay damages to Monsieur de Lauge in the amount to be assessed by this court as the worth of the lost fowl.

JEHANNE DUFAY: Ah, Your Honour, this may be justice, but it's hard to bear. I scarcely have means to feed my young ones with what my poor Gilles left to me—

MAGISTRATE: You should have thought of that, my good woman, before you let your animal run amuck.

GODBERT DE LAUGE: Heaven bless you, Your Honour. By the Virgin's snow-white bubs, you're a righteous man. Bless you. But these injuries, Your Honour. My tunic. My arse. Look at my missing finger. The hound must be punished!

MAGISTRATE: Be silent, stonemason. We are getting to that. It is the further judgment of this court that, for his crimes, the hound called Wolf shall be taken from this place to the potter's field, where he shall be whipped and then hanged by the neck until dead. And it is our will that his carcass be left on the gibbet for three days and nights as a warning to the other curs, before it is taken down and burned in the town ashpit.

GODBERT DE LAUGE: You hear that, devil? (Laughs and spits.) There won't be enough left of you to make a pair of gloves.

BUTCHER'S ROBIN (weeping and flinging his arms around the hound): Oh, Wolf. Poor boy.

JEHANNE DUFAY: My Wolf. Alas that your road brought you to me, if this was to be your end.

MAGISTRATE: Bailiff, take the hound away. Court clerk, what is the next case?

COURT CLERK: Guy-Bernard de Fauchefleur, wagoner and hostler, stands accused of carnal relations with a hor—

ADVOCATE BARTHÉLEMY: Your Honour, forgive the interruption, but I have a request. Clearly the hound can no longer live, at least not here in Le Puy des Choux. But I am willing to take him back to Paris with me and assume guardianship of him. I have a dog of my own at home, a most docile and loving creature, from whom I trust Wolf would in time learn gentleness and obedience.

MAGISTRATE: A generous offer, Maître. But there is no guarantee the hound would not continue its bloodthirsty ways, leading perhaps to worse consequences in such a crowded city. Our decision stands. For the safety of all, the animal must die.

ADVOCATE BARTHÉLEMY: As you decree, Your Honour. Might I then have a last moment with my client?

MAGISTRATE: A moment. No more.

ADVOCATE BARTHÉLEMY (turning to Wolf): I am sorry, hound. I pray your forgiveness for what they are about to do to you in their ignorance and folly. It is your misfortune to be a noble creature in a world of mere men. Both Aesop and Apuleius have fitting words for such an occasion, but alas, the magistrate will not allow it. Farewell. If you have a soul, which I doubt not, I pray it may find the eternal reward of the innocent.

WOLF (jumping up on the lawyer): Don't go! I like you! Let's play!

MAGISTRATE: Bailiff, take the beast away before he bites any more fools.

BAILIFF: Right away, Your Honour. Come along, mongrel.

WOLF: I don't like you. I smell turnips. Where are we going? I need to pee.

Good Dog

Here there was one rule above all, and though it went against his deepest instinct, he learned to act on it without question.

The humans who worked in the fields were not humans.

If they stepped out of line, if they bolted or tried to slip away, they were fair game.

Go-Between

A knock at the sitting-room door caused Captain Dash's ears to perk up expectantly and roused Miss Amelia Fairfield from her reading. Amelia put aside her book and looked up to behold, to her very great agitation, Mr Edward Thornhill of Whitecroft Hall.

If I may intrude, Miss Fairfield, he said.

Captain Dash's well-groomed tail began to thump against the chaise longue with traitorous enthusiasm. He warmly remembered his first meeting with Mr Thornhill, not long after that young, handsome, unmarried gentleman had purchased nearby Whitecroft Hall and moved in with his ailing mother and widowed sister. Most mornings Amelia's father took his daily constitutional on the downs, and often Captain Dash accompanied him, and it was on one of those walks that they encountered Mr Thornhill on horseback. The young gentleman introduced himself and invited them to Whitecroft Hall to view the renovations he had begun on that venerable pile.

On that occasion Mr Thornhill's hounds had treated Captain

Dash as an intruder and had chased and nipped at him, even roughly mounted him. Thanks to the timely intervention of Mr Thornhill, Captain Dash was merely shaken, not hurt, and both he and Mr Fairfield returned to Asperlea Park with a most favourable impression of their new neighbour. Captain Dash, in particular, had been so taken with Mr Thornhill that he had returned on his own the next day to see the young gentleman, and, it must be admitted, in the hope that his hounds would provide another of their rough welcomes. On his journey it had begun to rain and Captain Dash arrived at Whitecroft Hall soaked and shivering. The kind Mr Thornhill drove him home in his phaeton to Asperlea Park, where he reunited the anxious canine with his beloved mistress. Thus it was that Mr Edward Thornhill made the acquaintance of Miss Amelia Fairfield, and so one might say rightly that from the Captain's brave excursion had arisen all that followed.

Why, Mr. Thornhill, Amelia said frostily. This is unexpected.

Having lived at Amelia's side since puppyhood, Captain Dash was keenly attuned to her every mood and gesture, no matter how slight or fleeting, as well as the fluctuating bodily musk emanating from her person that only a being with his exquisitely sensitive nose was fully cognizant of. In essence he could read her just as she read a book. It was as if her deepest feelings lay before him like a page from a novel, and now, at the sight of Mr Thornhill, those feelings proclaimed, *Ah, Thornhill, I loved you so, but you were cruel and now I despise you, no, I do not despise you, I am indifferent to you and your charms, yes, that's it precisely, that is how I feel, I feel nothing at all for you any longer* (not true, the Captain registered), *I couldn't care less whether you come or go or fly to the moon* (also untrue), *and I must make you see that* (this, on the other hand, very true).

I do not wish to inconvenience you, Miss Fairfield, Thornhill replied, stiffly. But there are . . . matters that I wish to address.

Amelia's cheeks betrayed her with a flush, summoned (Captain Dash surmised) by memories of the disastrous events at

the ball that had led to the abrupt breaking off of their cordial relations.

Address to me, Mr Thornhill, or to my dog? Amelia asked with ill-concealed scorn.

Now it was the turn of Thornhill's noble visage to redden.

Why, to Captain Dash, of course, he replied, swiftly recovering his self-possession. I doubt he will be cavalier with me, despite his being a spaniel.

Amelia smiled coldly at this feeble jest (which she secretly found rather witty).

Indeed, he is no fickle companion, sir, said she, and addressing the Captain, added, No, you are not changeable, are you, my dear Dash? As the weather, and men, can so often be.

Thornhill's left eyebrow arched. (Captain Dash discerned how keenly that observation stung.)

Indeed? he said, and in turn spoke to the dog. Pray what conclusions, Captain, have you drawn on the subject of the inconstancy of weather and men?

Dash felt Amelia's fingers tighten in his fur.

The Captain, she said, has often opined that it is best not to trust in the faithfulness of either.

How fortunate for you then, Miss Fairfield, Mr Thornhill said, slapping his gloves against his thigh, that you have such a loyal and reliable friend. It must lighten the tedium of an unwished-for visit.

Dash felt the air in the room grow charged, as before a thunderstorm. In spite of himself he let out a whimper, uncertain what emotion it signified. Like Amelia, what the young gentleman expressed was clearly not at all what he felt.

Amelia stroked the Captain's head soothingly.

On the contrary, my dear Mr Thornhill, Dash greatly looks forward to company and wishes no one to feel unwelcome. Isn't that so, Dashy?

Perhaps in that spirit, Captain, Mr Thornhill said, you and your mistress would permit me to remain a moment longer.

A silence fell, broken only by the continued thumping of the spaniel's telltale appendage. These humans might strive to conceal their passions, but he would not. It was not in his nature to play such games.

By all means, Mr Thornhill, Amelia finally said. Dash would not have it otherwise. Please sit.

As he took a seat opposite Amelia, a look of relief momentarily flickered in Thornhill's galvanic blue eyes.

I shall call Betty to bring tea, Amelia said.

Thank you, but no, Miss Fairfield, Thornhill said. I will not keep you long.

As you wish.

Another silence fell, this one of the kind Captain Dash knew all too well—full of unspoken emotion held in to the point of pain.

I see you have a book, Miss Fairfield, Thornhill said at last, gesturing to the small clothbound volume at Amelia's side.

I have any number of books, Mr Thornhill. Reading is one of my favourite occupations. It is so enriching, I find.

Yes, reading is very... good. Is it a history, or a book of devotions, perhaps?

It is a novel, Amelia said.

Ah. I confess I've read very few novels. Give me the latest stud book and I am content.

Both handsome young people now blushed to the roots of their hair. Amelia was the first to recover her composure.

Then you have deprived yourself of a great many pleasures, Mr Thornhill, let me assure you.

Silence again descended. Captain Dash shivered with a kind of anguished delight. Living with such a nimble-witted young lady, he had come to savour the bite in words that carried hidden meanings.

What is the novel called, may I ask? Thornhill was struggling, like someone pulling a recalcitrant hound on a leash, to keep the conversation lurching along.

It is a new work by the author known only as A Lady, and it is titled *Sense and Sensibility*.

An elegant title. A diverting novel, I trust, Miss Fairfield?

Very.

The mysterious lady is a fine writer?

The finest I know of.

That is high praise. Perhaps I should seek out her work.

I encourage you to do so, Mr Thornhill. There is much you might learn about the hearts of the gentler sex.

Further silence followed, filled with unspoken suggestion, more awkwardness, tightened breathing. Fidgeting with gloves on the part of Mr Thornhill, and in Amelia's case the tightening of her fingernails in the Captain's flesh.

And how are you faring since last we met, Captain, eh? Thornhill said, leaning to chuck Dash nervously under the chin. Busy courting pretty poodles in the park, I should imagine.

Dash is too steadfast a soul for passing fancies, Amelia said, as she absently stroked the dog's sleek tail. Aren't you, my dear Dash?

Thornhill's gaze followed the delicate movement of Miss Fairfield's slender fingers, his throat bobbing as he swallowed.

An admirable quality, he said. When he finds the one spirited bitch who is his equal in all things, I am sure he will know it.

Amelia's breath caught, and Thornhill appeared taken aback by his own words. Remembering his meeting with that gentleman's brutish hounds, Dash understood very well both his mistress's alarm and her yearning to hear more in such scandalous vein.

Would that make Dash happy, do you think, Mr Thornhill? To have such a . . . partner in life?

It would guarantee fulfillment for them both, I am certain.

If one's native temper is fire it should be matched with fire, or neither party to a union is likely to be satisfied. From what I have observed of successful marriages, *happily ever after* is false to the skirmishes and conflicting passions which give spice to the many years that follow one's wedding vows. Only in novels do heroes, or heroines for that matter, rest contented with a nature unequal to their own for the sake of a facile conclusion.

About some novels, sir, you may be right, Amelia rejoined heatedly. But I imagine the author of this particular novel would agree with you about the concord of souls. At any rate, a dog understands better than most men do that true companionship is a rare gift and not to be spurned.

Dogs are indeed wiser creatures than we give them credit for, Thornhill said. And true friends are a blessing.

He turned to Dash. His face had suddenly gone pale. Something momentous was about to occur.

In that spirit, Captain, he stammered, if you would, please tell your mistress that I . . . I wish for nothing more than her . . . her friendship, that is. Indeed let me say that I believe I once enjoyed your good mistress's esteem, but lost it in a moment of rash and heedless disregard. An error I pray might not be fatal to my . . . hopes.

Amelia clutched Dash tighter. He was aware of her quickening heartbeat through the layers of lace and muslin.

Mr Thornhill, I . . . this is not . . . you mustn't . . .

Her face became so utterly bereft of colour that Thornhill half rose in alarm.

Miss Fairfield, I have caused you distress. I will go.

Dash suppressed a moan. Humans and their absurd niceties. It was time for him to express with his own person what they kept concealed (poorly, it must be added) from one another.

He hopped off the sofa where Amelia sat and went to Mr Thornhill, resting his head on the gentleman's knee and gazing up at him with soulful eyes.

Thornhill laughed and gently stroked the spaniel's floppy ears.

We are friends, aren't we, my good Captain, he said.

You are, Amelia said with a reluctant smile, her colour returning as she beheld the easy affection between the man and her beloved pet. Though I must say his judgement has sometimes been questionable. He once tried to befriend a hedgehog.

Ah, but that was a test of character, Thornhill replied brightly. To risk one's pride to seek the regard of another, despite the danger of being pricked and spurned. You were brave to try, Captain. Perhaps, given a second opportunity, things might go otherwise.

The eyes of the two humans met over the spaniel's wavy locks.

Have you been so pricked, Mr Thornhill? Amelia asked, and again her face flushed.

Entirely through my own heedlessness, that gentleman said. Any sting that was given was a just response to the blunderings of a fool.

Nay, Mr Thornhill, I am sure that is not true. I am certain the other party bears responsibility for her own hasty words. And desires pardon for it.

No pardon is expected or required, Miss Fairfield. I say so sincerely. And . . . devotedly.

Dash woofed in accord, and Amelia could not help but smile.

It seems Captain Dash is inclined to agree, she said. Aren't you, boy? You also wish that an affinity of warm regard may thrive again as once it did?

And might I dare to hope, Captain, Thornhill said, his voice low and fervent, that it might one day be more than friendship? Indeed that it may become, in time, a regard of the deepest and most profound kind. That is to say, in other words, what both parties would have no hesitation in describing, and more importantly knowing, in their hearts, to be . . . to be nothing other than the sentiment of sincere and ardent love.

Amelia turned her head away.

I . . . she faltered, that is to say . . . Captain Dash hopes so too.

With sudden resolve Thornhill took Amelia's hands in his. She did not protest. Indeed she turned her radiant eyes fully upon the gentleman, her bosom rising and falling.

Dash jumped between them, leaping and barking, and there followed laughter and joy, like the return of cheering sunlight after a shower of spring rain.

But here we must draw a curtain on the further intercourse of Miss Amelia Fairfield and Mr Edward Thornhill. Let it be noted, however, that Wolf (yes, dear reader, it is indeed he, under this rakish alias!) was entirely contented. Having played his part in the delicate rapprochement with the aplomb of a seasoned diplomat, he retreated to his favourite spot by the fire and curled up in its cozy glow. From this vantage he observed with canine nonchalance the swift lessening of distance between the two young people, and the unsuppressed ardour and esteem in their mutual gaze. As hands brushed and breaths quickened, Wolf sleepily shut his eyes and sighed, confident now that life at Asperlea Park would be enriched by the frequent presence of this gentleman who was so liberal with his jaunty greetings and belly scratches.

And if the continuing endearments in the drawing room were of a nature to make even a dog blush, well, we shall take comfort that our four-footed hero was the soul of discretion. He merely turned his back to afford the lovers their privacy, indulging himself in visions of abundant table tidbits, the well-earned reward of a successful matchmaker.

Underdog

A bunch of us dogs were huddled outside the Malamute
   Saloon;
Here in the snow it was fifty below, under a big icy moon;
While our masters sat by a roaring fire and tippled and
   kissed the whores,
We shivered and growled and occasionally howled; that's
   life for a mutt out of doors.

Koda, our leader, with ice on his muzzle, spoke up to be
   heard o'er the gale,
To pass these long hours while our masters carouse, let's
   each tell a tale from the trail.
We quickly agreed with a wag and a bark and settled
   down in the snow,
All eager to share the trials we'd been through, in this
   land where few dare to go.

Juneau went first, his proud coat once sleek, now matted, tattered, and worn:
My life, he said, was happy at first; to a proud Tahltan bitch I was born.
With the folk of the Eagle we lived and thrived, our bond both deep and true.
They knew our speech and our hearts, as we theirs: a fellowship shared by few.
Then came the rush, the lunatic lust for that shiny stuff found in the stream.
It brought the pale, haunted men to these shores, chasing a feverish dream.
They felled the trees, fouled the streams, the air, as if all was theirs to defile.
The Eagles who'd guarded the pass for an age had it plucked from them, mile by mile.
They saw their dear Mother beaten and stripped, for so they call the good Earth.
And some indeed joined in that pillage, plund'ring for all they were worth.
The newcomers brought with them burning drink that rang the Eagles' knell;
The spirit called Hooch that promised you heaven and plunged you straight to hell.
One day a sourdough offered a bottle to my human in trade for me.
Once the master I knew would have turned away from such ill-bred temerity,
But the palefaces' potion had worked its spell and pride had long fallen to shame;
He took the rotgut and handed me over; I was given a strange new name.
Since then I've pulled their wearisome loads o'er bog and ice and stone,

My paws are split, my spirit 'bout quit; I dream of a home that's long gone.
These men drive us dogs until we collapse, then leave us to die by the way;
I wish I knew why we must suffer this fate. That's all. I have no more to say.

Next up was Smoke, a husky so tough he'd hauled sleds when only a pup:
I've climbed dizzy passes and jumped crevasses, where other dogs simply gave up.
I've battled and beat both blizzard and bog, and thought these the worst I might face;
But I learned there are trials too hard for even the strength of our bold canine race.
My first master, a lad with gold-fever mad, came straight from a warm far-off city;
I hauled his kit up the cursed Chilkoot Trail that ne'er showed tenderfoot pity.
Rushing to doom he'd dragged me along; I was given no choice in the matter.
We lost the trail and wandered for days; like thin ice I heard his hopes shatter.
The weather turned foul; the temperature fell like the merciless blade of an axe;
The lad cursed and cried, then one night he died, and his flesh turned the colour of wax.
I watched o'er his remains for four days and more, as loyal a dog as you'd wish;
By then it had already been half a moon since I'd tasted flesh, fowl, or fish.
The ache in my belly ground my loyalty down, and at last I heeded its call.

What did I do? I'm sure you can guess. I ate the boy, mukluks and all.
It took me a week to crawl back to town. My arrival created no stir.
The man who'd lent me out only said, Back in the harness, you cur.

After him Lucky, a Newfoundland plucky, had a tale to chill flesh to the bone:
I've seen what gold can do to a soul when greed turns a man's heart to stone.
My masters were partners, blood brothers by pact, 'til they struck a rich vein one night,
The smiles soon died, the laughter turned sour, as they argued o'er sharing it right.
I watched in horror, my fur on end, as shouts turned to curses and blows,
Then one swung a pick and felled his friend; how quick the spilled blood froze.
The murderer trembled, his face ashen grey, as he buried his mate by the stream;
Then he packed up his stake and we hurried away with a sackful of metal agleam.
The prize brought him wealth, fame, and fine friends eager to milk his largesse;
But his cheeks grew hollow, his head sank low, like a weight on him sorely did press.
He'd squander and spend, trying hard to pretend that his fortune was honestly got,
But you saw in his gaze the sickness within, as that crime caused his spirit to rot.
'Twas on me he vented his conscience black; I suffered for his disgrace.

He starved and beat me; in winter's deep chill his door
   was shut in my face.
Now he haunts the saloon, all but a ghost, cash gone like
   dregs down the drain,
While here in the cold I watch as of old, for a master
   who'll ne'er come again.

Then up spoke young Champ: Men are just bad. I've
   known few worthy of trust.
I followed one once, a bad, brutal sort, who swapped furs
   for the twinkling dust.
So gentle he was with his husky team; the whip our poor
   backs oft caressed.
I gave him my all, and what's worse I knew I'd die for this
   man and feel blessed.
One night on the trail we heard chilling howls, and soon
   the source was revealed:
Wolves, a whole pack, were hot on our track; a sure bet
   our fate was sealed.
With carnivorous smiles they chased us for miles, but I
   led that rocketing sled
So fast o'er the snow the runners caught fire; the frozen
   tundra glowed red;
The sparks flew back and lit wolfish pelts; with yelps and
   howls of pain,
Those singed sorry beasts gave up the pursuit, ne'er to
   chase man again.
We thought we'd earned our keep all right, our musher's
   praise and thanks,
But curses flew from out of his hood and whip strokes
   kissed our flanks.
The bundle's straps had shaken loose and the furs were
   now strewn o'er the trail

For miles behind; to gather them up would mean hours of irksome travail.
The lout lashed us, the dogs who'd delivered his ungrateful hide from doom.
'Twas then that I knew no kindness I'd find from Man this side of the tomb.

You're right, growled a voice from out of the night, and every one of us bristled
As from the gloom slunk a dark canine shape, its fur all blood-caked and grizzled.
How long he'd stood nigh with nary a woof to warn us that he was there
We couldn't say; this great grizzled beast, whose scowl would frighten a bear.
If ever a pooch had Wolf in his blood, this chap had the most, I aver.
We tensed and bared fangs, but cool as a cuke he nudged into our circle of fur.

There's dogs you meet, on trail or street, who snag your soul like a hook;
And such was he, and he looked to me like a hound from some old storybook;
With a frame cruelly scarred and the wary regard of a stray without any friend,
Champ he addressed with a glacial stare: Did you get sweet revenge in the end?
Well, no, said the pup, I just ran off one day. It seemed the wiser decision.
The stranger's eye narrowed, but he spoke not a word of scorn or haughty derision.

———

Friend, Koda said, we've shared our plights, and the
    night has yet to pale;
So please, be our guest; we humbly ask that you tell us
    your own sad tale.

The stranger growled, Not worth the breath. You all
    know the dénouement.
What do we get for our hard, faithful toil? A loving kick
    in the jaw.
That's if we're lucky and keep our skin; more often
    death's our reward
For serving those who aren't deserving to be called a
    dog's master or lord.
In Dawson's delirious streets I once heard a man named
    London preach
Of something called true brotherhood, and how it's
    clean out of reach
For most of the fools who toil here, bound to cruel
    labour's shackles.
As he spoke his piece, my blood arose, all horripilate
    were my hackles.
He told of cities choked with smoke from whence the
    gold-mad hail
Who fled their own oppressors' yoke to seek this far-off
    grail.
From a man I learned that 'round the globe men suffer
    our own cruel fate,
Like dogs they're treated, lashed and driven, unless they
    change their state.
And some do rise. They bare their teeth, they howl back
    at tyranny.
They fight and die for dear freedom's sake, for peace
    and dignity.

———

The stranger paused, his voice gone hoarse with passion and with woe.
Not a word we uttered, nor did we stir in the thickly falling snow.
Of such things we'd not heard a peep before, nor had guessed the sorry lot
Of humans just as much as hounds by cruel Fortune's notice forgot.

And so, the stranger went on to say, I've spurned the company of Men.
I'll not be cursed or cuffed or beat or harnessed up ever again.
It's cost me blood to claw my way to freedom's bracing air;
But now I'm here, my brothers all, to ask whose soul will dare
To join me on my rebel road and scorn these servile ways,
Break free from leash and gun and be the master of your days;
No more to bow and cringe and beg, no more to knuckle under,
Spirit crushed and strong limbs spent for worthless human plunder.
That's my challenge and my hope: that you'll stand and join with me,
To cast down our oppressors, boys, and from our bonds burst free.

Despite the freezing dark, our hearts caught fire and started burning;
At the stranger's rousing words we felt deep down a fearsome yearning,

A mad howl that rose from the depths and threatened to burst like a flood;
And it seemed to say, Repay, repay, and we tasted our own bitter blood.
But just as quick the broil simmered down; our fire had sputtered out.
On everyone's face you saw only looks of confusion and of doubt.
You might have heard a mouse's blink, so quiet was the scene;
For all our gripes and unearned stripes, we were held by a tether unseen.
Man thinks he's tops, but in what truly counts, Dog is the superior;
We don't carry grudges or burn for revenge, despite our beastly exterior.
A kind of hunger's been bred in us that's not banished with scrap and bone,
It's the need to abide at our comrades' side; that's the place a sled dog calls home.
A good day's run, a spot by the fire, with the stars for a bright roof above;
That is all we desire and all we live for; some folks might call such a need love.
And that is why nary a peep was heard from our shaggy canine throng;
We cherished this cold, hard, miserable life that wasn't meant to last long.

The stranger saw that his summons had failed—none would answer the call;
He spoke no word of reproach but turned and plunged back into the squall.

As the swirling flakes took him, we all felt a pang for a life so wild and free,
Not worn out in service or bound on the wheel of some primeval decree.

As we settled back down to wait out the night, from the tavern a tumult arose
Of screams and shouts; we figured no doubt some drunkards had come to blows.
Then the lights went dark, and two gunshots blazed; men stumbled out into the cold
With a tale of betrayal, of hate and revenge that just couldn't wait to be told.
We shrugged and buried our snouts in our fur; such incidents happened quite often;
At dawn one husky or two from our crew would find their liege lord in a coffin.
For maybe a minute they'd be free from toil, but sure as the dancing Auroree,
It wouldn't last long; there's always more fools lured by a false golden story.
Tonight we dogs would dream, I knew, of humanless snow-mantled plains,
While the morrow would find us, just as before, happily bound in our chains.

Speak

Come. Sit. Stay.

Away to me. Look back. Hold. That will do.

Fetch. Shake a paw. Roll over.

Place. Heel. Release.

Watch me. Leave it. Settle.

Come on, boy, *speak*. You can do it. Speak. Yeah, that's it! Good boy!

For the love of all that's holy, would you shut the fuck up?

This is her mitten. She was wearing it. Take a good sniff, girl. That's it. We need to find her. You understand? Find her.

What have you got in your mouth? What is that? Drop it right now. Drop it. Drop it. I said DROP IT!

It's me, boy. It's really me. Look at you, poor old fellow. It's been such a long time, hasn't it? Too long. I'm sorry. I'm so sorry. But I'm back home now. I'm back for good. Let's keep that a secret for now, just between you and me. Nobody else needs to know I'm here. Not yet, anyhow. That's why I'm dressed like a filthy beggar. But you sniffed me out, didn't you. Of course you did. Faithful old friend. You can rest easy now. Just rest. I'm back and I promise I will take care of everything.

No, no, not there, oh my god, NO.

You're my little star. A star that collapsed into a black hole that sucks up all my money.

I offer you on the pyre of he who was your master and friend. Go now, and be swift. Run ahead to the sky people and tell them the great warrior, my beloved, is coming.

I would appreciate it if you'd stop rearranging the pillows.

No, that's not another dog, that's you. Yes, seriously, that's *you* in the mirror. It has to be. There couldn't possibly be another face like that in the whole world.

You are my woof-woof, my only woof-woof.
You make me happy when skies are grey.
You'll never know, dear, how much I woof you.
Please don't take my woof-woof away.

I'm not talking to you right now. And don't you look at me like that. You sit right there and think about what you've done.

Listen, society wants me to cut your balls off. It wants to deny you one of the primal pleasures of life as a mammal. They call this being a responsible pet owner. It's not really about that, of course. It's about control, like always. Society hates anything that evades its control, and your balls are a prime example. So we're going to rebel. We're going rogue. I promise you, sir, you're keeping your balls. And your dignity.

Okay, okay, I get it. Enough already. Yes, this thing sounds like a demon from hell that eats puppies. It's going to clean the carpet, that's all. I won't let it hurt you.

Honestly, if it wasn't for you, I'd be lying dead in a ditch somewhere.

When you stare at the wall like that it really freaks me out.

It's tinkle time, baby. Can you tinkle for me? That's it, baby. Yes. Look at you go.

We're leaving, girl. Yes, we are. Ssshhh, yeah, Mommy's whispering and that's weird, I know, but it's okay. Just keep quiet, that's a good girl. Such a good girl. I wish I had a chew toy for you, but I couldn't find the non-squeaky one. I promise I'll buy you the noisiest, chewiest toy of them all when we get to where we're going. There's the taxi at last. Thank fuck. Come on, sweetheart, get in the crate. That's it, girl. We're going somewhere good. I promise. Somewhere safe.

Do you love me?

Hello. It's nice to meet you. I wonder where you came from. That's a bad limp. Would you like to come in and have something to eat? It's okay, I don't bite.

After dinner we have to take the Dee-Oh-Gee to the park. The Dee-Oh-Gee is getting on my enn-ee-are-vee-ee-esses, aren't you, Dee-oh-Gee?

Oh, no, I just remembered. It's your birthday and I forgot. Can you forgive me?

How have things been for you today, pal? As for me, well, guess what, I lost my job. Yep. Fifteen years and boom, adios muchacho. I've been *offboarded*. That's the nice-sounding word corporate pirates use when they make someone walk the plank. The security guy marched me to the door with a cardboard box full of my stuff, in front of everyone, and the asshole actually said, *Have a nice day*. That's capitalism for you. No one's fault. Nothing personal. Just business. I'm telling you, pal, you don't know how lucky you are not to be a member of club *Homo sapiens*. We treat each other like dogs, if you'll pardon the expression. No, worse than dogs. I wouldn't dare treat you like they just treated me. If I kicked you to the curb, there would be howls of outrage and I'd be public enemy number one. So what are we going to do now? That's a good question, pal. What are we going to do?

You look so sad. Missing your mom, I bet. I'm missing mine too.

Well, this is it. The fateful package has arrived at last. I will now open it and we will discover just what you're made of. Exciting, isn't it? All right, here we go. Drum roll, please. Let's see now. Hmm. *Dog, male, four years old.* So far so good. *Labrador: 58 percent*. Well, that's no surprise. I knew that. Everyone knew that, you big goof. *Golden retriever: 32 percent.* Also not a major revelation, is it, Mister Instant-best-friend-to-total-strangers. *Shih Tzu: 8 percent*. No way. Holy Shih Tzu, some real kinky stuff must have happened up in your family tree, eh? Yikes. But let's not dwell on that. That's the past and it's not your fault. Lastly we've got *Undetermined: 2 percent.* Undetermined? I've never heard of that breed, have you? Well, it's just not true. You're the most determined guy I've ever met.

Hurry up and take a crap already you little bastard. I've got things to do.

Sorry, honey, but what's going on right now is a duo, not a trio. You'll just have to wait outside the door.

Adult male canine subject eleven-D-three. That's what it says here on the chart. Eleven-D-three. That's the designation they assigned you. You're not supposed to have a name. You can't have a name. They won't give you and the others names. You know why? No, of course you don't know. That's one saving grace. You have no idea what's coming. First they're going to cut your vocal cords so they won't have to hear your suffering. Then they'll harness you inside a cubicle and strap electrodes on your paws and administer electric shocks. They're going to do this to you day after day, and when they've learned what they want from torturing you, for no reason you'll ever understand, they're going to administer a lethal injection to you and toss your body in the incinerator like so much trash. All because you don't have a name. They don't have to see you as *someone.* You're adult male canine subject eleven-D-three. Actually, you're not even a subject, are you. You're an object. I can't stop them from doing what they're going to do to you. I'm so sorry for that. But there's one thing I can do. I'll let you in on a secret. I give all of you who come through this place your own name. I do. *They* don't know. It's just for you and me to know. So your name is Eddie. Do you like it? And I'm Lena. I'm going to be looking after you, Eddie. You and me, Eddie and Lena. I'll be here for you, I promise, right to the end.

Listen to me good, you ugly fucker, I paid a fortune for you. They told me you were a champion, a born killer, so you're getting back in that ring and acting like one, you hear me? This is it, one more round for the whole pot. Finish it now. GO. Go for the throat. Yes, that's it. Yes. Yes. YES. Fucking *end* him.

You know what, I'm going to call you Ranger. I hope you like it. Ranger was the name of my last dog. He passed away three years ago from an osteosarcoma. That was really hard. When I lost Ranger I thought that was it for me. Ranger was one of a kind. Irreplaceable. And your lives are just so short. It's not fair. It's a guarantee of pain and loss, that's what it is. So I was done, I told myself. I was going to be alone from now on, and that was okay. I was learning to accept it. Then I met you. I wasn't even looking. I was helping my sister pick out a puppy for my nephew, for his ninth birthday; that was all that was on my mind. Ranger, the first Ranger, was a chocolate Lab. Different breed, colour, size from you. Different sex, for that matter. Pretty much everything different. But when I came into the kennel and you popped your head up and gave me that look . . . You recognized me. I know you did. And I recognized you. I don't know how much of Ranger there is in you, but I know there's something of him. I can feel it more strongly now, with you and me in the car. We're almost home, Ranger. That's where we're going. Home.

Tell me how you're feeling, baby. I can see something's wrong. Just tell me, so I can help.

What is so goddamn fascinating about this particular patch of grass? Does it have some magical aura that all the other patches of grass don't have?

The St. Bernard is done napping and gets up off his bed. The St. Bernard sniffs the human's pant leg and gets a scratch

under the chin. The St. Bernard pads over to his bowl on the off chance something might have been put in it while he was dreaming of rescuing mountain climbers from avalanches. Alas, the St. Bernard discovers to his chagrin that the bowl is empty. The St. Bernard looks at the human as if to say, *Why are you sitting there narrating my every move when this bowl needs filling?* The St. Bernard knows who's the boss in this relationship. Neither the human nor the St. Bernard harbours any doubts about that. The bowl gets filled. The St. Bernard eats. The St. Bernard finishes, takes a drink of water, and pads over to the screen door to look out at the street. The St. Bernard gives a perfunctory *wuff* as a delivery van goes by. The St. Bernard paces back and forth in front of the door a few times, on the off chance that a walk might be in the cards. One isn't right now, sadly, because the human has to finish this boring-ass paperwork. The St. Bernard sighs, flumps down like a sack of potatoes, and curls up at the human's feet. Time for nap number two? Stay tuned to find out.

Poor boy. Poor sweetie pie. You know why you can't jump over the hedge anymore? It's because you're getting old, my love. You're catching up to me. I'm already there. Neither of us ever thought this would happen. We were going to be young and strong and beautiful forever, weren't we? But it's okay. We'll go hand in paw, you and me, as our teeth fall out and our bones crumble to feta. We'll face this together.

I'm coming right back. Honest.

Daddy's widdle wuvvee-poo. Daddy's widdle boopsy-boo.

Let's see now. *The Lovers.* Hmm. *The Queen of Cups.* Ah. And . . . *the Moon.* Well, well. This is an auspicious spread. The day looks to be a fine one for you, madam.

Are you happy? I wish I could know for sure.

PLAY

    Not right now, buddy.

PLAY

    I said not right now.

PLAY

PLAY

ANNA PLAY

ANNA PLAY WOLF

    I said *not now*, okay?

ANNA ANGRY

    I'm not angry, I'm just . . . forget it.

ANNA SICK

    I'm fine. Can we just drop it?

VET HELP

    Jesus. I don't need a vet.

MEDICINE GOOD HELP ANNA

    Yeah, well, wouldn't that be nice if it did.

ANNA SMELL

    Great. My dog thinks I stink.

ANNA SMELL SICK

    Can we change the subject?

ANNA PLAY

    It's not gonna happen, pal. I'm sorry. It's not fair to you, I know.

ANNA PLAY WOLF

ANNA HAPPY

ANNA NO SICK

    Fuck! You know, I'm starting to wish I hadn't trained you to use these goddamned talk buttons.

ANNA ANGRY

    Not at you, buddy. I'm sorry. It's not your fault you can't speak Human. The problem is, I can't speak Dog.

ANNA SAD

Yeah, well, you got that right. Life sucks sometimes. Shit happens, as they say. And there's no happy ending.

WOLF NO FETCH ANNA SPEAK

No fetch Anna . . . what does that mean?

WOLF NO FETCH ANNA SPEAK

You're talking gibberish now. Oh. Wait. Oh my god. You . . . you mean you don't get it. You don't understand.

WOLF NO FETCH ANNA SPEAK

Oh my god. Okay. okay. I owe you the truth. Let me try. Let's see. This is so hard. *Me.* Anna sick. You were right. Anna *sick.*

ANNA SICK BAD

Yes, but more than just sick. Big sick. More sick.

MORE SICK

Yeah, that's it.

WOLF SAD ANNA SICK

Yeah, well . . . that makes two of us.

WOLF HELP

Oh, sweetheart. You can't help me with this one.

WOLF LOVE ANNA

This is one of those things love can't fix, honey.

ANNA REST

I've been resting. It's not going to be enough. I'm dying. My cancer came back, and this time it's terminal.

WOLF NO FETCH ANNA SPEAK

I know. I know you don't understand. How can I put this. Anna . . . broken.

ANNA NO BROKEN

Yes, I am. Anna broken.

ANNA BROKEN FIX

Some broken things can't be fixed. No, no fix.

NO FIX

That's right. I'm going to leave and I won't be coming back. Do you see? Anna go.

ANNA NO GO
ANNA STAY
I wish I could. But Anna go. Not now. But soon. Anna go.
WOLF GO ANNA
You can't come with me this time, buddy. No Wolf go.
WHERE ANNA GO
It's hard to explain, sweetheart. Anna go . . . sleep.
ANNA SLEEP
Yes. Anna sleep. No get up.
ANNA SLEEP GET UP
Not this time. No. I'm sorry. Anna go sleep, no come back.
ANNA STAY
I want to stay. More than anything.
ANNA STAY
Honey, I wish it was up to me, but it's not.
WOLF SCARED
Yeah. Me too, buddy. Me too.

I'm sure there's a heaven just for dogs and you're tearing the place up right now, aren't you. You had way more soul than most people I know.

Tracks

Scent

Wolf lived a quiet life in the heart of the city with his owner, a famous author who wrote at night and who suffered from allergies and other neurasthenic ailments that kept him mostly at home. When the author did venture from his door he went out of his way to avoid other people. In consequence Wolf got taken for walks at odd hours and had rarely met others of his kind.

Most of the time he would lie on the rug by the author's desk, drowsing and waiting patiently while the author scratched the itch called writing. Wolf usually had a better sense of when it was time to take a break than the author did. He was something of an expert on narrative himself, after all. He understood you've got to have variety and action, a change of scene every so often. Characters shouldn't just sit around. Something has to happen.

Something rarely did, living with the author. There were no deep friendships, no romances, no exciting encounters for Wolf or his owner. Their outward existence was one of long habit and reassuring routine.

Only through his nose did Wolf live other, more eventful lives.

He would step out eagerly into the grey predawn streets, the author tightly clutching his leash and shrouded in an oversized hat, coat, and scarf, no matter the weather, so that people in this nosy city wouldn't recognize and pester him. The air was purer during these empty hours—the day's miasma of sewer gas, street dust, and industrial fumes had yet to obscure all other smells, and the traces of canine life Wolf cared about stood out all the more clearly. Each lamppost, tree, and fire hydrant held the phrases, paragraphs, and entire chapters of an ongoing saga that was his alone to read.

At the first corner a fresh mark on the sandstone facade had been left by Patch, the high-strung, yappy terrier from two blocks down. Wolf detected acrid notes of stress hormones and the cherry flavour of the patent calmative that Patch's owner had been futilely adding to his meals for weeks now.

Next they passed the ornate wrought-iron fence that Eleanor, the old French bulldog, favoured. Her aged trickle was weaker today than usual—lately Wolf had detected that something in her blood was not right. Wolf whimpered softly as the author tugged him away from the fence. Eleanor had been a constant in his rounds for years now, the wise and revered matriarch of the neighbourhood. He feared this change foretold her final bow.

Next came the ample splattering of O'Malley, the Rottweiler-boxer mix, his mark richly odoriferous and assertive as always. He had been scrapping again with that yappy little mongrel from several streets over, that was plain. O'Malley's owner, a pugnacious retired policeman, fed him raw steak and spoke to him in hard, unloving monosyllables. (Wolf had overheard him many times from the author's apartment window.) O'Malley was a major player in Wolf's ongoing chronicle, big and gruff, with a touch of the rogue, but underneath, a faint whiff of cowardice that might one day be his undoing.

Near the park, on a crumbling curbstone, he sniffed a pungent drop or two from Beatrice, the standard poodle, whose owner's frantic attempts to keep her away from other dogs were to little avail. The bitch's alluring scent intertwined with Carl's, the big, oafish mongrel from across the street. Beatrice had recently come into heat and Carl was bewitched. A budding amour, it appeared, was in the wind. Wolf himself had been castrated at a young age—for him Beatrice's seductive bouquet was simply information.

Wolf always made sure he left his marks well away from the others', not out of a sense of superiority but simply so that he wouldn't contaminate the others' traces with his own. More than once on these morning walks Wolf had glimpsed his fellow canines. He'd heard their owners speak—and shout—their names. But he felt no need for their company. What they left behind was more than enough. He often pondered how unlike most of his own kind this made him. After all, what did your typical dog truly desire, more than anything else in the world? Other dogs, of course.

Day after day, walk after walk, Wolf sniffed and surmised, threading together the lives and loves and antagonisms of dogs he'd never laid eyes on. Their joys, sorrows, rivalries, and alliances—all made a script for his hypersensitive, refined nose to read. He felt Patch's anxiety and O'Malley's hidden insecurities. He monitored Beatrice's ongoing rejection of Carl's blundering advances, and mourned as elders like Eleanor faded away.

Then it was time to return to the confines of the author's apartments, where he would spend his day alone in a suite of stuffy, thickly curtained rooms lined floor to ceiling with corkboard so that the author could sleep without the street noise disturbing him. It was here that Wolf dozed and replayed the lives and loves and losses of the neighbourhood's canine denizens, often weaving in imaginary twists and complications of his own creation. It was his life's work. His *roman pipi*.

One thing he never did was to place himself in his chronicle. He was the observer, nothing more.

So things went until one chilly spring morning, when something new appeared in Wolf's world.

He almost missed it. Only the faintest trace remained at the base of a lamppost, nearly washed away by a puddle of soapy dregs dumped by a window cleaner. But there was enough, just enough, to make him pause, nose twitching, nostrils flaring in and out, raking in every last odour-bearing particle. The author pulled softly at the leash. Wolf ignored it. The author tugged harder. Still Wolf clung to the phantasmal scent.

The maker of the mark was a male. Young. Healthy. Vital. Not from around here. And beneath that new and startling scent lay something else. Before he was yanked away Wolf had time for one last deep inhale, enough to let the layered smells both concentrate and unravel their secrets within his quivering snout. At the fore bloomed a heady musk that made the fur on the back of Wolf's neck stand up. And, beneath it, that hint of something even more compelling, a hazy vista of vanishing odours, green and warm and summery. This elusive underscent made his heart throb with a kind of rapturous agony, and in an instant he knew it for what it was.

The past.

His past.

He was tiny again, in a dim corner of the barn, nestled against his mother's side, wrapped in her scent of warm, soft fur, milk, earth, and comfort. He could feel her heartbeat next to his own, steady and reassuring, thrumming through his small body. The soft hair of her underbelly tickled his nose, and he burrowed closer, seeking the familiar nubs of her teats. The sweet, rich nectar of her milk filled him absolutely.

Around him squirmed the bodies of his littermates, their feeble yips and whines mingling with his own. His bigger and

stronger brothers, pushing to get the best latch at feeding time. The sweeter smell of his sisters, their fur downy soft against his. Sometimes the others would crawl over him, their clumsy paws pressing into his ribs and belly as they jostled for position, but he didn't mind. He didn't yet know himself apart from them.

And beyond the cocoon of his family, the farmyard, shaded by great dark trees. The rustle of mice in the hay. The cluck and squabble of chickens. The dungy aroma and low moaning of the dairy cows needing to be milked. From farther out came the tang of sweating horses and the alarming racket of their neighs. Sometimes the breeze would bring dust kicked up by their hooves and he would sneeze, his whole body convulsing.

At night came the ceaseless chirring of crickets. The distant hooting of an owl. The air cooled and the night wind carried the humid scent of dew-damp grass and unknown nocturnal animals venturing out to hunt. He would snuggle closer to his mother for comfort against these disturbing visitations from another world and fall asleep.

The humans brought strange new fragrances, including that of soap, which he didn't like, and cooking, which he did. The loud voices of the humans frightened him at first, but he soon got used to that and eagerly crawled toward them when they came into the barn. Their paws were big and sometimes clumsy when they scooped him up and held him, but the way they stroked his fur was soothing.

Each day, as he grew, there were new discoveries. The first time his eyes blinked open to golden sunlight slanting through the barn slats, its beams full of swirling motes. The morning he took his first wobbling steps out into the open air, alarmed at the prickly grass beneath his paws. The terror of coming face to face with a big barn rat and fleeing back to his mother.

Beyond all of this, though, lay something vast and elusive that heralded itself with faint tantalizing smells of sun-baked earth and unmown immensities of grass. Grasshoppers and butterflies. The perfume of sagebrush and the dry, dusty aroma of chaparral. And most alluring and frightening of all, he could hear and smell the fierce, untameable creatures that roamed out there wherever they wished. At night their distant roars and shrieks echoed across that dark unknown, so far away and yet so thrillingly near.

One by one his siblings were taken away, until only he remained. Then rough hands came for him, too, tearing him from his mother's side. Her frantic barking pierced his ears, growing fainter as he was carried away. The scents that had been his world were suddenly gone. He was somewhere else, in a wooden crate within a small, vibrating space, smelling horse manure, hearing the rattle of harness and the steady clop of hooves. After a long time the sounds outside became louder, harsher. Voices shouted, locomotive smokestacks chuffed wheels rattled and squealed.

He had been brought to the city. To a pet shop on the busy shopping boulevard. He hadn't been there very long before the author came hurrying in, muffled up in coat and hat, muttering something about his doctor telling him he needed exercise. The author took no time at all in picking out Wolf from the other puppies, as if the choice didn't matter, and he took him straight home to his apartment, with its bottled-up air and insulated walls. Wolf was young enough that he soon forgot everything that had come before. His mother, his siblings, the ranch. And the mysterious place that lay beyond.

Beyond was where the strange dog had come from.

As the days went by Wolf became obsessed with tracking the mysterious canine. His marks appeared sporadically and always in unexpected places. Sometimes just the faintest hint, other times a bold pronouncement that made Wolf start and whirl around, as if the maker of this fearless signature was still there, ready to pounce.

He knew that the other dogs were also aware of the interloper. Patch's anxiety spiked. O'Malley's growing fear spread to other dogs. Beatrice yearned for the phantom male and Carl grew discouraged and gave up his courtship. But Wolf knew that these messages from the edge of the world were not intended for the other dogs. They had been left for him alone to find and read.

Wolf's soft bed by the radiator now held no comfort. The familiar kibble in his dish no longer provoked his appetite. He lost interest in his chronicle of the neighbourhood dogs. Their lives were so constrained, so predictable, and, he now realized, so utterly boring. Patch would get more and more neurotic until dementia claimed him. O'Malley's fear would lead him one day to bite someone who dared pet him, and then it would be off to the pound to be destroyed. Carl would regain his ardour and go on pursuing Beatrice without hope of satisfaction. As for Eleanor, she had never done anything unexpected or impulsive, anything truly *doglike* in her entire pampered life.

Worst of all, the same was true of him.

There was only one remedy.

One morning the author opened the door to his building before he had clipped the leash to Wolf's collar. This was the moment. Wolf dashed away into the street and kept running, his owner's frantic shouts growing fainter and fainter.

He couldn't have said where he was headed, other than south.

Wolf passed through the city market, where farmers arriving from the countryside were unloading their wagonloads of fresh fruit and vegetables. This gave him the first clue. With his nose he followed the farm wagons and carts backwards through time, along their night journey from homestead to market. The fading scent of the wagons, their phantom wheels rolling and bumping in reverse, brought him to a road that led to the outskirts of town and into the countryside.

The sun rose and cast his shadow beside him, lean and long-limbed. His nose followed spilled grain on railroad tracks, a cabbage fallen off a cart, the muddy hoofprints of cattle that had been driven to the slaughterhouse the day before. They all led the same way. South, into the sun.

Wolf trotted on. He drank from puddles. A pheasant killed by a hunter but fortuitously unretrieved furnished his noon meal. He rested for a time in the shade of a thorn tree and then went on. The scent was overwhelming now. Wolf quickened his pace, nose to the earth. His own scent had changed during his journey. The stale fug of his daily life—his flannel bedcover, tobacco smoke, axle grease, the effluence of thousands of humans, the dim, fusty presence of the author—had been washed away by sweat and dust and a single thought.

South.

He passed farms. One of them might well have been the place where he had been born.

That no longer mattered.

He left the road, crawled under a barbed wire fence, and loped along a track recently made by draft horses. Then he left even the fences and the traces of hooves behind. The land was flat and still, the air grainy with dust and pollen. Wolf descended into a narrow gully where a shallow stream chattered over stones. Lapping at the shockingly cold water, he tasted the distant mountains with their armour of ice.

When he climbed up the far side of the gully he knew he had arrived. Before him stretched the great sea of grass, infinite, eternal.

And there before him also, as if it had been waiting since the first day of creation, stood a dog. Tawny of fur and amber-eyed, it regarded Wolf without stirring a muscle. The hot breeze of the plain carried its scent to Wolf. And the scent spoke to him and said, It is time.

This might be the dog that had left its markings in the city for him to find. It might be one of his own brothers. He could

imagine it: His siblings had been taken away one by one, but they hadn't all gone to the city. Some had stayed on the farm, to live and work there. At least one, this one, had been given—like an offering—to the great plain. Taken in by the taciturn, sun-leathered men on horseback who dwelled there, themselves only half tame. Devoted to a brief, harsh life of chasing and fighting other dogs, the wild dogs and wolves that preyed on the drifting white flocks. To sleeping outside on the cold earth and hearing the footfalls of night beasts prowling at the edges of the camp. To live the swift years in a hot, dreamless fury and then to die and become the grass.

But the possibility that this dog was the mysterious leaver of markings, or his own sibling, seemed unlikely to Wolf now, given the immensity that lay before him. Whether the stranger had lured him and waited here for him or whether their paths had crossed by pure chance was no longer important. What mattered was that he had come. He had stepped into the role that had always awaited him. At last he would be a character in his own saga.

The other dog threw back its head and howled. Wolf felt the sound echoing and rising in his chest and let his own howl loose, tearing his throat, searing his lungs.

He stepped onto the plain and his old life closed behind him like a door.

As he approached his waiting adversary, one final, new and yet ancient scent came to him. The cold breath of fate. The plain had given him this gift and it must be accepted. Only one dog would walk away from the encounter.

Wolf broke into a run. The grass hissed and he felt the wind ruffle his fur, saw the sunlight glint off the other dog's bared fangs as it sprang to meet him. He sensed the hot blood in them both, ready to leap forth at the first bite of a tooth.

There on the plain, under the savage sun, his chronicle reached its end.

Breeding

6:00 a.m. Wolf wakes in his orthopedic bed, specially designed to support his delicate spine and alleviate pressure on his neck and back muscles. His personal assistant, Sebastian, gently rouses him with an affectionate Good morning, Your Excellency.

6:15 a.m. Sebastian presents Wolf with a small bowl of porridge specially formulated for his sensitive digestive system. With tiny toy breeds of Wolf's rarefied bloodline, it's common for the canine intestinal tract to be cramped and prone to disorder.

Wolf washes down the meal with the finest distilled water.

6:30 a.m. Exercise. Wolf enjoys a gentle regimen of stretches and limb rubs in the palace spa, administered with practised virtuosity by Sebastian. The regimen helps manage his hereditary joint problems and maintain his mobility.

Sebastian used to take Wolf outside the palace grounds for walks, discreetly accompanied by secret service agents, of course. Then one day a disturbed man threw a brick at Wolf and screamed hurtful things about how a fucking dog lived better than most of the people and by God a reckoning was coming. Wolf didn't eat or sleep well for days and Mummy decided there would be no more walks outside the palace compound. She had the security forces search for the man, but he was never found.

7:00 a.m. After exercise Sebastian presents Wolf with his "soup," a blend of fortified bone broth and herbs for his arthritis. Wolf's immaculate pedigree, traced back by the palace historian nearly two hundred years, has bequeathed him certain physical challenges he must struggle with every day. But as Daddy always says, especially when unpopular decisions must be made, like raising taxes or conscripting more men to fight his wars, greatness is not for the faint of heart.

7:20 a.m. Wolf selects his accoutrements for the day from an array put before him by Sebastian, employing his snout to opt for a smart lavender bow tie and a silk vest that helps regulate his body temperature, given his breed's tendency to catch dangerous chills.

7:40 a.m. Toilet time. Sebastian takes Wolf out into the palace courtyard for his morning necessaries. As he finishes, an attendant hurries to scoop up what Wolf has left and discreetly dispose of it. Mummy and Daddy appreciate a pristine view whenever they happen to glance out a window. The palace veterinarian once suggested to Mummy that the sterile courtyard might not be good for Wolf's mental health. The man actually used the word *sterile* in both Mummy's and Wolf's presence. He found himself replaced that very day with a new vet, although Mummy has since made sure that carefully selected small toys, treats, and other objects of canine interest are placed in the courtyard every morning for Wolf to find.

8:00 a.m. Wolf joins Mummy as she takes breakfast in her private apartments. He sits on a silk cushion at her side and sips a kidney-supporting herbal tea while Mummy munches toast and reads the morning briefs out loud, usually with approval but sometimes uttering a dismayed sigh.

8:30 a.m. Mummy departs for her daily engagements, giving Wolf a loving pat on the head. Wolf settles into his favourite spot by the window, surrounded by his collection of soft, easy-to-grip toys designed for his weak, prognathic jaw, another inheritance from centuries of selective mating and refining. On the walls are portraits in oil of family dogs who have passed on—each one the gold standard of its breed, each one in its day sparking a craze among the elite to own one just like it, each one long gone, felled by the price that must always be paid to scale the heights.

9:00 a.m. Sebastian takes Wolf for his daily swim in the palace pool, which helps soothe his dermatitis and maintain his muscle tone without putting undue stress on his fragile limbs.

10:00 a.m. Wolf visits the new palace vet for a routine checkup to monitor his congenital heart murmur. He stumbles descending the stairs on the way there, and Sebastian has to help him. Wolf's whiskers are regularly trimmed, which causes him some minor spatial uncertainty, but Mummy doesn't like his whiskers getting too long and unruly. When left untrimmed, Daddy jokes, they make him look like an anarchist. Mummy doesn't find this funny.

11:00 a.m. After another quick trip to the courtyard, it's time for the first nap of the day.

12:00 p.m. Noon meal. Sebastian serves Wolf thin slices of chicken breast, brown rice, and steamed broccoli, selected to support his urinary tract and prevent the formation of kidney stones. It's all fresh—absolutely no canned food is allowed in Wolf's diet; its presence would be horrifying, given the rumours of how it's made. It's a dog-eat-dog world everywhere but here, Daddy teases, much to Mummy's dismay.

12:30 p.m. Therapy. Wolf attends one of his twice-weekly sessions with his canine psychologist. Currently they are working to manage his anxiety when parted from Mummy, and his fear of loud noises. Lately there have been more gunshots and police sirens than usual in the streets outside the palace.

1:00 p.m. Social hour. Just as Mummy has her coterie of friends chosen from the cream of society, Wolf has three carefully selected canine companions with whom he spends time. One is a huge mastiff from the palace guard, another a wire-haired pointer that often accompanies Daddy on stag hunts at one or another of his vast private preserves. The third companion is even smaller than Wolf (this is important), a pocket-sized Pomeranian belonging to Mummy's younger sister, who stays alone in her suite in the palace now and never goes out, ever since the man she loved turned out to have revolutionary sympathies and was sent to a re-education camp in the far north.

The other dogs are required to be on their best behaviour: no tussling with, bullying, or biting Wolf, as befits their lower rank. They each can sniff Wolf's behind, once only, but Sebastian has been ordered to prevent Wolf from sniffing theirs.

For all of them, including Wolf, the social hour is simply no fun at all.

2:00 p.m. Nap number two.

3:00 p.m. Wolf joins Mummy on the central balcony for the weekly public appearance. As a special treat, Daddy, back from his tour of the new armaments factory, accompanies them. Wolf sits proudly on an elevated stool made just for him. At Mummy's urging he waves a paw at the wildly cheering citizens assembled in the public square below. His eyesight being what it is, he can't make out faces that far away. But his presence is a must, since Wolf is by far the most popular member of the First Family. The people genuinely love him. They find it ironic and funny that so diminutive a pup has such an intimidating name. That Mummy and Daddy are also physically unimpressive and yet command an entire nation might be considered equally ironic, although no one would dare find it funny. A newspaper cartoonist is currently in prison for drawing the comparison.

The palace photographer makes sure to get some great shots of Wolf with his paw in the air. As always they will be retouched before being released to the state media, to edit out the benign but unsightly wart on Wolf's jowl.

4:00 p.m. Afternoon toilet. On the way, Wolf has an accident in the corridor. These days he often doesn't make it to the courtyard in time, a lapse for which Sebastian has been chastised by Mummy twice already this month. Sebastian swiftly delegates cleanup and carries Wolf to the playroom, engaging him with an array of clever puzzle toys made for dogs, designed to keep his mind sharp and slow the progression of his breed's predisposition to mental decline.

5:00 p.m. Tea. Wolf joins Mummy on the terrace. The day is sunny and warm. Fighter planes roar overhead and Wolf restrains his urge to run and hide, whimpering just a little. Mummy rewards him for his courage with one of her own creamy vanilla eclairs, a treat he is not supposed to have. It'll be our secret, Mummy whispers fondly.

6:00 p.m. Dinnertime. Wolf joins Mummy and Daddy in the echoing dining hall. He tucks into his meal of raw salmon shaved Bible-paper thin, more steamed broccoli, and pumpkin purée, all chosen to support his sensitive stomach and prevent diarrhea and bloating.

Mummy and Daddy seem distracted and ill at ease with one another this evening. Daddy speaks not a word until Mummy asks him what's the matter and he erupts, turning red in the face, raging about the incompetence of his administrators, the paltry number of arrests his secret police have made lately despite all the signs of a serious conspiracy in the works, and to top it all off a protest over food prices that's erupted in the provinces and has yet to be put down. With a mortified glance Mummy reminds Daddy not to use the words *put down* in Wolf's presence.

Daddy knocks his wineglass onto the tablecloth and storms out.

Wolf cowers under Mummy's chair.

7:00 p.m. After dinner Wolf receives his daily eye drops and ear cleaning to manage his breed's propensity for vision and hearing deterioration. Along with his weak eyesight, Wolf doesn't hear as well as he should. He sometimes mistakes sudden noises and motions made by the serving staff for threats. He has nipped more than one new maid who moved a little too hastily while tidying up Mummy's apartments. Considered in a positive light, however, these attacks have helped Mummy weed out the undesirables in her employ.

7:30 p.m. Wolf settles onto his own plush sofa, built low to the floor so that he can climb onto it without help, a boost to his self-confidence. Sebastian dims the electric lights and plays a gramophone recording of soothing natural sounds designed to calm Wolf's restlessness and promote restful slumber. Wolf enjoys one last diet dog treat.

8:00 p.m. Sebastian tucks Wolf into his bed with his favourite soft blanket and a fan switched on to help mask any external noises. When night comes there are always external noises, many of them distressing.

2:07 a.m. Wolf wakes to an unexpected sound. The door of his room opening. Is it an assassin? Is it the screaming man? He's too petrified with fear to summon a bark.

It's Mummy. Relief, and confusion. This has never happened before. Wolf wags his stub of a tail and Mummy scoops him up and sits with him in her arms on the low sofa. She talks to him softly, telling him all the things she's never said to Daddy. About how Daddy has become so angry, so distant, so preoccupied with work. She blames the people out there. Their unrest and rebelliousness have forced Daddy to neglect his home life to deal with them. How they seem to hate her, too, when she has tried so hard to be like a mother to them. How ungrateful they are. How unreasoning. They're like animals. Low-born brutes. But at least she has Wolf. Wolf is her baby. Her protector. Her joy.

Wolf is delirious with happiness, but deep down inside a question itches at him: Is it good or not, Mummy's unprecedented visitation? Will it happen again, and if it does, what will that mean?

To cap off this wonderful but unsettling night, Mummy tells Wolf a bedtime story. It's a fairy tale about a noble king and a gentle queen and how their brave and handsome pup saves them from the monsters that threaten the kingdom, and how everything turns out all right in the end. As fairy tales do.

Stay

He was lost.
    After a meagre dinner of fried cod, peas, and leftover potatoes, they had stepped out for some fresh air, the older woman, the younger woman, the child, and him. It was a warm, quiet evening and many humans and their dogs were out enjoying a stroll.

Then the sirens had started up.

During thunderstorms, Wolf fled to the coal cellar in abject terror. It didn't matter if they were storms of rain or this new kind of storm, the one heralded by a siren that made the family go silent and hurry outside to the shelter that the man had dug in the yard before he went away. Wolf knew only blind panic and the frantic desire to be down in some kind of den, tunnel, or hole. Somewhere under the earth.

But he and his humans weren't at home when this storm came, and he couldn't escape to the cellar.

They were on a busy street when the sirens began their horrible wailing. He had gotten thinner these last hard months and so, when he tugged on the leash in fear, his collar slipped off. He didn't think—he just ran, darting this way and that in panic among the many humans scurrying for shelter. When he thought to look for his own, they were nowhere to be seen, heard, or scented.

Then, through all the hurrying legs, he caught a waft of chill air and found stairs that led down under the earth. He didn't hesitate.

The long, dim space at the bottom of the steep steps was already crowded, humans clustered on the platform, leaning against the walls, hunched on cots. He threaded his way among them, ignored or frowned at, looking up into faces in the desperate hope of finding one he knew.

An old, uniformed human with a megaphone was walking up and down the platform, urging everyone to keep calm and stay where they were. No one seemed to be paying him any attention.

Wolf slunk through the crush of bodies and finally found a place to cower between a wall and a crowded bench.

The storm broke.

The booms were distant at first, then they began to march closer. He stood it as long as he could, and then he sprang up and moved on. There had to be somewhere deeper, somewhere the thunder couldn't reach.

He came to an area where homeless humans had established their territory with curtains of laundry, crate tables, and hot plates for tea. The smells of long habitation greeted him: stale bedclothes, fried fish, tobacco, piss in dark corners. In one alcove formed of boxes and suitcases four unshaven older men were playing cards. Two teenaged girls were practising the latest dance and shrieking giddily at their mistakes.

There was noise here. Welcome noise that almost drowned out the thunder.

Then he saw the young woman.

She was sitting on the edge of a lower bunk, nearly swallowed up in a man's coat that had the acrid reek of cigarette smoke wafting from it. She noticed him looking at her and smiled. It was enough of an invitation.

He approached, tail lowered.

Are you lost? the young woman asked.

He panted, his throat parched with fear.

You can sit with me, the young woman said. I'm lost too. We'll make a fine pair.

There was a muffled boom directly above, followed by a long, rolling shudder. A child screamed as the platform shook and dust sifted down from the tiled roof. The young woman's hands gripped the edge of the bunk. She gazed up at the ceiling, biting her lip. There was no space to climb onto the cot with her, so he set a paw on one of her hands.

She looked down at him and smiled again.

Aren't you the cheeky one, she said. I've got an unfortunate fondness for your type.

Another close blast rocked the tunnel, then another, farther off. The humans around them, even the teenagers, had gone silent.

Looks like we're in for it, said a plump woman at the other end of the cot, with young ones sleeping around her. You all right, love?

Never better, the young woman said, but her voice quavered a little.

The older woman's tone, and then his own nose, told him what he hadn't noticed at first. He thought of the child at home and instinctively moved closer, sniffing at the gap in the coat.

That's right, she whispered to him. Carrying a little extra baggage these days.

Above their heads, sirens wailed on and thunder rolled.

The young woman wiped at her eyes with the sleeve of the huge coat.

What am I going to do? she said. I can't go home like this.

She gave a weak laugh.

Any ideas, Casanova?

He panted and gazed up at her as if she had the power to stop the terror. He understood that this kind of storm was made by humans. Which meant they must be able to make it go away.

The roof shuddered under another impact and the lights fluttered and winked out. For an instant all was silent in the sudden blackness. A male voice said, If that don't bleedin' tear it, which raised a few scattered laughs. Then a wavering chorus of Mummy, Mummy, Mummy began, up and down the tunnel.

The darkness didn't bother Wolf. It felt safer. But the young woman reached down and put her arm around him. She was shaking. He licked her hand.

Slowly the bombing drew off into the distance. After a long time a woman's voice spoke matter-of-factly into the dark.

I've got your cuppa, Agnes.

Thank you, dear, called another woman.

A babble of voices now began in the dark, as if the mention of tea had been a magic spell. The beam of an electric torch appeared far down the tunnel, then another. The wardens were bringing lights.

It would be safe now to go back up, into the open air.

He climbed to his feet.

Leaving so soon? the young woman said. Her eyes were wet and puffy.

He stood in front of her, hesitating. He had to go, he had to find his humans. He needed to get back to where he belonged. Home.

Two ships in the night, she said. That's my luck all over again.

He looked away, down the crowded tunnel, then back at her.

He sat down at her feet.

It was an impulse as deep as the one that had brought him here. When a human was in need you went to them. You offered the only thing you had, which was your presence.

What do you know, the young woman said. Chivalry isn't dead.

She reached out and scratched him between the ears.

The young human had sought shelter here for the same reason he had. There were other reasons he didn't understand, but he had heard them in her voice.

He would stay for now.

Curriculum Wolfae

Rival, camp watcher, companion, cave warmer, big-game hunter, herder and flock protector, temple guardian, idol, boundary walker, gatekeeper, psychopomp, healer, scapegoat, sacrifice, dinner, street survivor, sled puller, indentured labourer, farmhand, long-distance hauler, outcast, pariah, emperor's sleeve warmer, tiny tame lion, icon, invader, trespasser, prey, pointer and retriever, royal gazehound, king's brachet, bear and bull baiter, turnspit, truffle sniffer, racer, comforter and lap-warmer, source of clothing, guide and follower, tax collector's muscle, tracker, wolf hunter, fox harrier, sworn enemy of coyote and jackal, dogfighter, cowboy, courier, gamekeeper's deputy, alpine rescue professional, bargehand, water rescue ace, intimidator, artist's subject, young lady's confidant, estate guardian, captain's mate, bird-setter, decoy, ratter, night warden, accomplice, carriage rider, pest control and pest, garbage disposal and garbage, punching bag, wolf in the fold, haunter of graveyards and corpse-eater, cadaver finder, filth, plague-bringer, moon-mad monster, unreasoning brute, soulless automaton, soldier, military asset and collateral damage, refugee, fugitive, vagabond, migrant, clown and circus performer, shill, fire station mascot, chaperone, athlete, seeing-eye escort, hearing assistant, actor and movie star, hero, sidekick, villain, crony, subject of sentimental song, Heinz 57, national pride, fetish, phobia, mine and bomb sniffer, search-and-rescue worker, contraband and contraband snooper, customs inspector, security detail and law enforcement, eugenics experiment, death row inmate, disputed asset in divorce case, abductee, inheritor, seizure alert expert, food and drug tester, astronaut, drag performer, model, impulse purchase, chattel, trophy, blueblood, showfreak, designer accessory, vogue, craze, media celebrity, biohazard, therapist, cancer detector, rescue(r), distant relation, honorary human, friend, fur baby, life partner, family, shadow, person, mirror.

Laika

Stage One

There was a small window in the capsule, no larger around than a food dish. From time to time a human would look in at her through the window. They would smile and wave.

She shifted in the tiny, cramped space, waiting for them to let her out.

They were not letting her out.

Her ears twitched at the muffled sounds beyond the walls of the capsule, the clatter and growls of the humans' machinery. In the past she had endured being shut up in a capsule much like this one for hours on end, for days on end. She'd gotten used to the solitude and the lack of space to move around in. But this was different, somehow. Those days had been practice, she realized. *This* was what the practice had been for.

She had already eaten all the food they'd put in the capsule when they sealed her inside. That was days ago. Since then, the humans hadn't brought any more. Once a tube had snaked into the capsule through the wall and refilled her food receptacle with water, but the water was long gone. She was so hungry. So thirsty.

There had been so many changes in her short life. She remembered the streets—the endless search for food, the fights with other strays over scraps, the humans who shooed her away with brooms and harsh words, the packs of shouting boys who chased her and threw stones at her. But there were good memories too—the kind babushka who left out bowls of soup, the children who would pet her when she followed them for a while on their way home from school.

Then came that night, after which nothing was the same. The man with the net, the rough cords tightening around her, the prick of the needle. She had fought, but her starved body was no match for the drowsiness that pressed down upon her.

She was brought to the long room with all the cages. There were other dogs here, some friendly, some not. The humans in white coats had fed her better than she had ever eaten in her life. She remembered Natalya, with the gentle hands. And big Dmitri, who almost never spoke but radiated calm and trust. Dmitri had come with her on the noisy flying machine that had brought her to this endless steppe. He would return soon and take her out of the capsule and quietly call her a good girl. Then they would go home, to the dog place. They would see Natalya again, and the other dogs.

There were more clanks and vibrations, then silence. Nothing happened for a long time. At the dog place there had been the endless tests, the noisy machines, but also the praise and pats and belly rubs when she performed well. She had been cared for, cared *about*. Dmitri or someone would come. They had to. Someone always came.

A sudden jolt made her yelp. It was followed by a climbing rumble that vibrated through her bones. This was it, she sensed. The moment all those puzzling days, good and bad, had been leading to.

An obliterating roar crushed her back into the padded capsule wall. She had trained for this too, spun for hours in an enclosed space, but again this time was different.

The tiny window blazed with searing fire.

The roar filled her head, shook her teeth, rattled her skull. Her heart pounded as if it would burst from her body. A force far stronger than the life in her body bore down on her, crushing, relentless. She gasped and struggled for breath, remembering Dmitri's soothing voice before the spinning practice.

Good girl. Just breathe. It will be over soon.

Suffering metal groaned and banged. The engines screamed. Her stomach lurched as the capsule shuddered and jounced like a living thing. She vomited. The inside of the capsule grew warm. Too warm. Panting brought no relief. She voided her bowels into the diaper inside her flight suit. She had never done that before, even when they made her wear the diaper all day at the dog place. Someone would come, they had to, to clean her.

The roar and the shaking would never stop. It would never stop.

It stopped.

It was over.

Silence.

Wolf felt something tug at her. Something she couldn't see or smell was trying to lift her out of her seat. She saw droplets of her own spittle drift slowly past her snout, like raindrops that had forgotten how to fall. This was so strange. She had come to someplace she had never been before. Maybe no one had been here before.

In the small, round window, the edge of a huge, glowing blue ball appeared and spun slowly, out of reach even if she had wanted to play with it. Was that what the humans in white coats had sent her here to do? The night before they had brought her to the capsule, the boss of the white coats had come one last time to visit her, and then he had done the unexpected. He had taken her home with him. To his little girl and boy, who shrieked with delight on seeing her. They played with her all evening and she curled up with them in bed for the night.

She had thought this was the final reward for all she had endured, all her hard work. Then before dawn the boss had brought her back to the room with the cages. And from there Dmitri had flown her in the noisy machine to the steppe. After they'd arrived and were on their way to a new building with a new room of cages, she had smelled vast open space and heard, far in the distance, the howl of wolves calling to one another. They were calling their own names across the dark: *Here I am.*

Frost was forming now at the edges of the capsule window. Wolf licked at it. This was water, it was cold, she could soothe her swollen tongue.

Her breath made fog on the glass.

Once it had cleared, she looked out at a blackness spangled with tiny specks of ice. She had never seen so many of these specks, never imagined their true multitudes, their hard, unglittering light. There was a cold out there that was not the crisp white cold of the streets in winter. This was a cold without smell or taste. This was a cold that ate everything and never ended.

And yet, in the capsule, there was only heat. Stifling. Crushing. Inescapable.

Her heart throbbed weaker and weaker. She felt herself shrinking, curling up inside herself like a dry leaf, the life in her growing smaller than one of those tiny lights. It would wink out soon and there would be nothing but the dark.

Home

Dawn lit the fence tops of a suburban backyard. Wolf stirred and stretched in his doghouse, his chain clinking softly. He'd been dreaming about a strange dog with fur that shone like the sun. Follow me, she'd said. And he'd followed.

The scent of bacon and eggs drifted from the house, along with the Beatles' newest hit jangling from the radio and the voice of Mother humming along. Wolf began to drool.

Teenager came out the back door, sleep and dreams still in her eyes. She crossed the yard, her ponytail swinging.

Hey, boy, she said, and unclipped Wolf's collar. He followed Teenager into the house and down the hallway to the kitchen, where the rest of Family was finishing their breakfast. His customary bowl of morning kibble was waiting and he got right to it. When Mother wasn't looking Little Brother fed him a piece of peanut butter and jam toast.

Father sighed and set down his coffee cup.

Welp, off to the wars, he said. He patted Wolf's head as he passed by with his slight limp, a keepsake from his service as a young man in the great conflict overseas.

Mother called him back.
You forgot. Again.
She handed him his lunch box.
Thanks, honey.
A peck on the cheek and out the door he went.

The children were next to leave, Little Brother chattering to Teenager, who paid him no attention. They made it to the sidewalk just as the school bus pulled up.

At last Mother, still humming, her apron dusted with flour from the cookies she'd already made for next week's PTA bake sale, opened the front screen door for him. Wolf took a last lick of his dish and bounded to her.

Off you go then, she said. And try to stay out of trouble.

A plastic bread bag covered in coloured dots skittered across his path, bobbing and pirouetting on the wind like a living thing. Without a second thought he was off, chasing after it.

The bag tumbled end over end. Wolf bounded in pursuit of his quarry, along picket fences and over lawn jockeys, ignoring Mrs. Nowicki watering her prize petunias and even the mail van trundling past.

Left onto Oak Drive the bag veered, Wolf hot on its trail. It caught for a moment on a fire hydrant, and he lunged, jaws snapping on empty air just as a contrary gust wafted the bag once more out of reach.

Down the hill they went. Wolf's tongue lolled as he ran, his ears flapping like flags. Past the Mister Softee ice cream truck he sprinted, not even tempted by the sweet scent of waffle cones.

The wind fell away and, with a leap, he brought down the bag at last. He chomped at it for a bit, then left it and wandered away. It was only a bag, after all.

Under the trees at the park some unusual humans lounged on blankets spread across the grass. Their clothes were loose-fitting, their hair long and tangled. It was strange for humans to sit

around outside this early in the day. Wolf decided to investigate.

One human with a scruffy beard was strumming a guitar and singing about someone named Alice who was ten feet tall. Next to him a female with daisies woven into her long hair was threading beads onto a string. The others were passing around a bottle of some funny-smelling liquid and chatting quietly.

The guitar player noticed Wolf first.

We've got a visitor, he said drowsily.

With cautious steps Wolf approached.

The human with the daisies in her hair reached out, offering Wolf a piece of ham from a sandwich.

Hungry, pup? Here you go.

Wolf accepted the offering. The meat was about to go off, just the way he liked it. The odd outdoor people watched him as he gulped it down, all smiles.

He's got a collar, said one of the other humans, his eyes concealed behind round, blue-tinted spectacles. He must be somebody's dog.

We're all somebody's dog, said the guitar player. We just took our collars off. He'd do the same if he could, wouldn't you, pal? You can teach them to heel and beg, but underneath all that jive, man, dogs are rock and roll.

I wonder if he's lost, the daisy human said. Her voice was soft and dreamy in a way that made Wolf lower his guard. He reclined at her feet, at ease but just alert enough to be ready to bound away in case things were not as they seemed.

He doesn't look lost, the guitar player said. He looks like he's right where he belongs.

I am, Wolf said, figuring it was worth buttering these humans up in case another piece of sandwich might be on offer.

What did he say? asked the blue-spectacled human.

He said, *That's groovy, man*, the guitar human said, and laughed. Are you a groovy pooch, dude? You better not be working for the pigs.

Don't tease him, the daisy human said. He's a sweetie. You're a sweetheart, aren't you?

Wolf basked in the attention and the gentle scratches under his chin. These raggedy humans were unlike most of the people he met in his daily wanderings, hurrying everywhere and, if not downright hostile, with no use for him. He sank into a kind of stupor, forgetting about home for the moment.

Then a new scent caught his attention. The spectacled human was holding out a small brown piece of something that smelled like dirt and moss.

Here, man, this'll expand your furry mind.

Wolf snapped the brown thing up and licked his lips.

Tell me you didn't just—! the daisy human shouted at the spectacled human. Are you freaking stupid?

Don't be a drag. It was just a little piece.

You don't know what that stuff's gonna do to him.

Hey, dude, the spectacled human said to the guitar player, tell your old lady to get off my case.

She's right, man. That was not cool.

Jesus, it was just for fun. Man, I thought you cats were happening, but you're a couple of squares.

At least we're not assholes, the daisy human said.

Ah, fuck you.

No, fuck you.

The peaceful mood had been shattered. Wolf scrambled to his feet.

Now look what you did, the daisy human scolded. You scared him. It's okay, pup.

But Wolf was already leaving.

Smells were all wrong. Things looked too big, or too small. Sounds had taken on shapes he could see. A car's horn streaked across the sky like a bird of prey. The rumble of a distant train made goosebumps appear on the pavement.

Something was after him. Something he had to outrun. So he ran. He ran and ran until he came to a place he'd never been before.

There were fewer houses here. A broken gap in a leaning fence of splintery wooden slats caught his eye. It was dark on the other side. Wolf squeezed through.

On the other side of the fence, rusting shells of cars and trucks lay amid tufts of grass and spiky thistles on the gravelly ground. The sharp scents of oil and decaying metal formed visible tendrils in the air, something that had never happened before. Smells didn't do that. But these ones did. The tendrils swirled and reached out for him.

Wolf frantically tried squeezing himself behind a big tire that was leaning against a truck's bumper.

The tire shifted and rolled away over the bumpy ground. It wobbled and finally fell over with a boinging wallop that sent little white rabbit-shapes hopping around.

From behind a stack of oil barrels a huge mastiff with a massive jowly head loped into view. It stopped and looked at him with its one bloodshot eye. Where the other eye should have been was a hole.

Well, well, said the mastiff. And I thought this was going to be a boring day. Who are you?

The mastiff's raspy voice came out in sharp, knife-like shards that flashed through the air.

Nobody, Wolf said, lowering his tail and avoiding the other dog's eye. Nobody at all.

Well, Nobody At All, you're just in time for brunch, the mastiff said.

That's kind of you, Wolf said. But I can't stay.

But you simply have to, the mastiff said with an ugly grin. You're the main course.

Wolf spun and bolted, darting between piles of rusted junk,

which closed around him. He heard the mastiff pounding the dirt after him. Where was that hole in the fence? The mastiff's huffing breaths were hot on his tail.

The skeleton of an ancient panel truck appeared just ahead, half buried in the earth. There was a narrow gap between the truck and the ground. Wolf scrambled through it just as the mastiff slammed into the chassis with a grunt.

The mastiff clawed at the hole with its huge paws, then stuck its muzzle into the gap, but it couldn't squeeze the rest of its head or massive body through. Wolf was safe, for now.

You're mine, the mastiff laughed. I can wait you out.

He began pacing back and forth in front of the little cave where Wolf lay panting and shaking. What was he going to do? He squirmed around in the tight space but could see no safe way to escape.

A skittering sound caught his ear. He turned his head just in time to see a sleek furred body dart up into the dark interior of the truck.

Mice. There were mice here. They probably had a nest somewhere. Wolf turned on his back and clawed at the wooden floor above him. The boards began to splinter. He got his fangs working on it too, and soon a large chunk came away.

What are you doing in there? the mastiff growled. Damn it, I can't see a thing.

At last Wolf shoved his head through, into the truck's interior, and tore at the seat stuffing.

A horde of mice came boiling out as he barked and snapped. They skittered everywhere, and some fled out the gap under the truck that he had squeezed through. He heard the mastiff wuff in surprise and then tear off after this new quarry.

This was his chance. Wolf squirmed out from under and ran for the fence. He sniffed along it frantically and came to the broken slat just as the mastiff came back.

I've got you now, it roared, and lunged.

Wolf lowered his head and crashed into the slat. It swung on its remaining nail like a trap door and he was through. From behind him he heard a wet crunch as the jagged top of the slat collided with the charging mastiff.

The big dog yowled in agony.

My eye! Oh, oh, oh, my poor eye!

Wolf didn't look back. He ran.

I'll find you! the mastiff blubbered. Nobody fucks with me and gets away with it! Ooooh, my eye! You hear me? Nobody!

The sky clouded over and the wind picked up. A few drops of rain began to fall here and there, darkening the pavement.

He was safe from the terrible dog, but something was still after him. It was in the raindrops, which now had a voice.

You'll never get home, the voice said. I won't let you. You'll never see your family again. You'll wander forever.

Hours passed as the rain swept in gusts and waves. World had returned mostly to how it was supposed to be, but Wolf had lost any trace of the way back to Family.

Hello there, a sweet voice called.

A woman in a flower-patterned dress stood at the gate of her picket fence.

Come on, the woman said, beckoning to him. She had something in her hand. A dog biscuit. A big dog biscuit.

Wolf padded over cautiously.

That's it, the woman said. This is for you.

Her voice was kind. She wasn't Mother, but she was close enough for now.

She set the biscuit on the ground for him and he devoured it while she stood watching with a smile. She smelled like flowers, but not real flowers. This was the canned flower smell Mother sometimes sprayed on the bathroom sink and tub. Unlike most friendly humans the flowery woman didn't try to pet him. In fact she seemed to be keeping her distance. That was all right, if a little odd.

Poor thing, the woman said, what a mess you are. She looked both ways, up and down the street. No one else was around.

Come in out of the rain, she said.

The woman led him inside her house. There was a sheet of plastic on the floor just inside the entrance and everything smelled of the same not-real flowers, with a hint of lemon. The place was shiny clean. It wasn't like home at all, but he felt safer here than outside in the rain.

The woman made him stand on the plastic sheet while his fur dripped rainwater, then led him to the gleaming kitchen, where she gave him some water in a bowl, from a jug she took out of the refrigerator. He lapped it up. Even the water didn't taste like proper water. It was so *clean*.

The woman sat down on a kitchen chair and patted her leg.

Here now, she said.

Wolf came over and sat at her feet, alert and ready for whatever else she might give him.

The woman leaned forward and quickly unclipped Wolf's collar and set it aside on the kitchen table, which was draped in some kind of crinkly paper.

There we go, she said in her lilting voice. That's better, isn't it?

Yes, it's much better, the woman said before he could reply. You don't belong to anyone now. Funny, isn't it, how people consider dogs their property, then they let them wander around doing whatever they please. It's like leaving your soiled underthings in the street for all to see. They'd be ashamed to be caught doing that, but it's perfectly fine for their four-footed property to leave messes on the sidewalk and dig up people's gardens and spread disease. You've been doing some of that today, I'm sure, you naughty boy, haven't you. Well, that's all in the past now.

Wolf suddenly felt sleepy. He lay down, panting heavily. His eyelids began to droop. The floor and the woman's legs became blurry.

Yes, the woman said soothingly. Rest now. No more wandering. No more dirt and filth. Just a beautiful, obedient, perfect dog, forever.

The strange dog with the shining fur was there with him, in a dark place.

Get up now, she said. This is no time for a nap. Follow me.

Wolf struggled up and the shining dog led him through a narrow tunnel that climbed steadily to a spot of light at its end. As the shining dog reached the light she vanished.

Wolf was back in the flowery woman's house. He didn't know how long he'd been asleep, but when he opened his eyes the woman wasn't there.

He got up, sniffing, wondering where she had gone. There was a faint scent of something that wasn't fake flowers, coming from a dim hallway. A trace of the outdoors, of dirt and fur and his own kind. It was weak, almost not there, but it *was* there.

Wolf slowly padded down the hall to a door at the end and nudged it open with his snout.

There were dogs here. Many dogs. On tables, on shelves, mounted on the wall. Dogs frozen in the act of begging, shaking a paw, running, jumping.

Perfect dogs. Forever.

The woman was there too. She turned. She had a long needle in her hand that she was flicking at with a finger.

Oh, she said. Bad dog. You weren't supposed to see this.

Her sweet voice had turned cold. Wolf growled in his throat and lowered his head, ready to lunge if she came any closer.

Easy now, the woman said softly, reaching into a pocket in her dress. Here, let me give you another treat and we can have a pleasant chat about all of this.

Wolf backed out of the room, snarling. Then he turned and ran to the front door. It was shut. There had to be another way out. He dashed into the kitchen and slid out of control on its polished linoleum, smacking a haunch on the refrigerator.

The woman appeared. She had a treat in one hand and the other hidden behind her back.

There, there, she crooned. You must understand. I'll look after you like no one else will. You'll never be hungry, cold, or sick ever again. Doesn't that sound nice?

Wolf inched toward the woman.

That's it, that's a good boy, she said. She bent forward, lowering her palm so that the treat was almost in reach of Wolf's snout. Her other arm stiffened.

Wolf pretended to go for the treat, bracing his back legs on the floor. When the woman had leaned forward just the right amount he jumped up and licked her face.

Ahhh! she screamed, flinging up both hands to push him away. The needle flew across the room and skittered under the table. The woman wiped frantically at her eyes and mouth.

You filthy, horrible thing, she screamed, falling onto her behind. You disgusting animal!

Wolf quickly edged past her. He felt cool air on his fur and found a landing, and at the bottom of it another door with a screen instead of a window. A moment later the door had no screen.

Wolf was gone.

It was coming down in buckets now. Raining dogs and dogs, as Father would say in this kind of weather.

Father. Where was he? Where was Family?

Wolf came to a busy freeway. Cars and trucks sluiced past, leaving a slashing spray in their wake.

On the far side there was an indistinct yellowish shape. Was it the shining dog? It had to be. She could help him.

Wolf waited for a break in the rushing traffic and dashed across.

A huge truck loomed suddenly out of the wet, its grille like bared fangs. Wolf bounded for the far curb as the truck swept past. The wind of its passage swatted him off his feet and he tumbled and slid down the wet embankment, then hit water with a splash. The shock of the cold drove the air from his lungs.

The creek, swollen with rainwater, tugged at him, clutched at him, threatening to sweep him away. Wolf paddled frantically, struggling to keep his snout above the waves. He fought against the current, aiming for the far bank, and at last his paws touched rocks and he was able to haul himself up onto the grass, where he collapsed, sides heaving as he gulped in air.

As he lay there, gathering the will to move, he heard a small gasp. Raising his head, he came face to face with a young human in a yellow raincoat. Her eyes were wide.

It was around here, Daddy, the girl said.

Wolf was in the back seat of the girl's father's big, fast car. The girl had her arm around him and was looking through the window. Looking for something or someone.

When he'd crawled from the water the little girl had coaxed him up the bank to her house, which was not far away. After what had happened at the flower lady's he was suspicious, but he could tell there was no guile in this new, small human. He was too weak to resist, anyhow. If there was any chance the girl could help him get home, he had to take it. The girl's mother and father had scolded her for going to the creek by herself, but they quickly got over it when they saw Wolf shivering and miserable in their yard. They'd dried him off with towels and given him a piece of roast chicken to eat. When he'd rested for a while on a blanket on the kitchen floor, the father had led him into the car and the girl had climbed in beside him.

Wolf understood they were taking him home, or at least that they wanted to. They just had to find it.

Are you sure, honey? the father asked. I think we've driven down this street already.

Yes, I'm sure. It was near the park. That's where I saw him before, I know it.

Okay, we'll go around this block one more time and then I think we'll have to head home. We can take him to the pound tomorrow. I'm sure someone's looking for him.

Oh! There, Daddy! There he is! That's the dog's boy!

The father pulled his car over the curb. The girl opened the door and jumped out. Wolf came after her.

There was Little Brother, who stopped and stared, then came running.

Just look at you, Mother said, hands on her hips. You lost your collar and you're such a mess I hardly recognize you, you ragamuffin.

Wolf wagged his tail. Mother shook her head and smiled.

Well, get in here then. You've had enough fun for one day.

Wandering Cloud

In the sweltering terminal of Palonegro Airport near Bucaramanga, a medium-sized black-and-white dog appeared one Tuesday morning, as if she had materialized from the collective sighs of a thousand tearful partings. No one could remember when she had arrived, yet there she was, weaving among the feet of hurrying travellers, sniffing hopefully at creased pant legs and swishing skirt hems. Eventually she curled up beside a potted palm and stayed there.

She was young, probably no more than two years old, with the sleek coat and bright eyes of a cherished pet. Everyone who saw her assumed she was *someone's*, a service dog, perhaps, who had gotten lost in the crowd and whose owner was looking for her and would claim her at any moment.

When that hadn't happened by the end of the day the airport staff debated what to do.

We can't kick her out, said Macario, a baggage handler who lived with several dogs of his own. She's clearly waiting for someone. They must mean to come back for her.

Yes, but why did they leave her here in the first place? asked Consuelo, who sold arepas from a kiosk in the main hall.

No one had an answer to that. Consuelo brought a dish with water and half a chicken arepa to the dog. Here you go, pobrecita, she said. The dog snapped up the tasty morsel and half-heartedly wagged her tail.

Stooping to study her collar, Consuelo didn't spot a name tag or any other identification.

If only we knew what to call her, she said. Then she might not feel so alone.

In the days that followed, the dog remained in the terminal, roaming the halls, looking up into the faces of travellers, most of whom hurried past, ignoring her, although a few took a moment, even from a frantic rush to catch a flight, to pet her. They would ask the dog what she was doing here and where her owner was, as if they expected an answer.

When the dog was still with them after a week, Consuelo said, We need a name for her.

Wolf, said Macario.

Wolf? exclaimed Consuelo. She doesn't look anything like a wolf.

I know, but it seems right.

How about Nube Viajera, suggested Evander, who cleaned the toilets.

Wandering Cloud, said Consuelo, pondering. Where did you get that name?

It's a song, said Evander, and he launched into a quavering rendition. *Return to me soon, my love, my wandering cloud. It is only for you that I live.*

Wandering Cloud it is then.

———

For thirty days and nights, Wandering Cloud lived at the terminal, leaving it only to go outside and relieve herself. Each day when arriving and departing passengers flooded the halls she would go on her solitary patrol until, worn out once more, she would return to her chosen corner, where Consuelo kept a water dish and food bowl for her.

She became a fixture. Pilots and flight attendants on their way to work always took a moment to greet her warmly. Children gave her licks of their ice cream cones. Travellers set bites of sausage and empanada before her like offerings.

Macario made a sign that he put up in Nube Viajera's corner.

Do you know this dog?

After a month had gone by and the dog's owner had not returned, Wandering Cloud's health took a turn for the worse. Her eyes, once bright with hope, grew dull and listless. She no longer bothered to raise her head when the sliding doors whispered open, and she refused all offers of food. Consuelo and the others took turns sitting with her, shocked by how she was fading away before their eyes.

Someone made a call and a veterinarian named Sotomonte came to examine Wandering Cloud.

Her owner must have abandoned her here, he told the gathered crowd, or she would have gone looking elsewhere. I believe this person must have seen the busy terminal as the perfect place to get rid of a pet they no longer wanted. Or perhaps they were emigrating to another country and left her here, thinking someone would adopt her. Either way, the dog has finally given up hope they will return for her.

His diagnosis: a broken heart, that most unscientific yet universal of ailments. Working in an airport, one saw it all too often.

The veterinarian called an animal rescue society to take the dog to a shelter. They arrived with a carrier and soft voices. The gaunt, weakened Wandering Cloud went without resistance, her spirit as spent as her body.

At the shelter they did all they could to revive her. Nutritional supplements and medicines were administered by intravenous drip. The staff spoke to her soothingly, telling her of the good home that surely awaited her if only she would eat, if only she would fight.

When the news of the dog's death reached the airport, Consuelo lit a candle in Wandering Cloud's corner. The flame wavered, like the wag of a tail, each time the doors slid open. For the staff it would remain one of the unsolvable mysteries of a dog's existence in this world—of anyone's existence, really: how someone so beloved that you would die to lose them could also be so heartless.

Unleashed

The abandoned shopping mall loomed before them, an ominous shadow against the red evening sky. Melody clutched the tire iron, knuckles white with tension. Beside her Wolf padded silently, his presence her only comfort in the lifeless wasteland that had once been a thriving city.

They crept through the mall's gaping entrance. Moonlight filtered through broken skylights, laying nightmare patterns across the debris-strewn floor. They passed overturned kiosks and fallen mannequins in shattered shop windows. Melody failed to notice that the mannequins' heads had been gnawed beyond recognition as anything human. Wolf also missed what the mannequins revealed—his keen sense of danger had become unreliable under the circumstances.

I think we're finally safe, Melody said to her companion. Good work finding this place, Charlie.

Just then a creak and a low moan came from somewhere deeper in the mall.

Must be the wind, Melody said.

The moaning grew louder. Wolf's hackles rose and he began to snarl.

Shit, Melody said. Not here too.

Out of the darkness they emerged into the conveniently overhead moonlight. One, two, three shambling, rotting figures. Clothes hanging in tatters, flesh peeling from bone, eyes black and empty of any feeling except a mindless, insatiable hunger.

Fuck, Melody breathed. This is not good.

She backed away slowly, with Wolf at her heels. As she turned, more shuffling horrors appeared, cutting off their escape.

The only thing for sale at this mall was a one-way ticket to hell.

Melody brandished the tire iron.

Come on then, fuckers, she said grimly. Come get some.

Wolf brushed up against her and she looked into his eyes. At that moment something passed between them. A decision. A goodbye.

Oh, Charlie, Melody breathed. No.

Wolf threw himself at the nearest walking corpse, his teeth sinking into strands of foul necrotic flesh and tearing easily through neck bones the consistency of blue cheese. A head fell to the tiles and shattered like a watermelon, followed by the rest of the creature's skeletal remains.

As it toppled Wolf was already leaping at the next one.

Charlie! Melody screamed. Charlie, watch out!

Wolf weaved among tottering bodies with grasping claws, twisting, evading, attacking. Drawing their attention away from Melody. Soon the horde's lifeless eyes were fixed solely on the dog.

Wolf paused for an instant to look back at Melody. In his eyes she read his final farewell, and one desperate urging: *Go.* Then he bounded into the darkness, and the nightcrawlers shuffled and lurched after him.

Melody backed away toward the entrance, tears streaming down her face. As she stumbled out into the cool night air, an agonized howl tore through the silence until it was suddenly cut off.

The mall stood silent, a tomb now for the bravest friend she had ever known.

Cut! the assistant director shouted. That's a wrap.

The lights went up.

Wolf padded out of the spot behind a green screen where he'd sat concealed, waiting until the scene was over. Extras in gruesome prosthetics got up off the floor and sauntered over to the refreshment table, chatting with each other about their golf game. The actor playing Melody slumped into a waiting chair and dug out her smartphone.

Wolf plodded off the set, half-heartedly accepting congratulatory pats from several members of the crew. In his trailer he flopped down onto his plush bed. His favourite chew toy lay beside him, but he couldn't be bothered to touch it. He sighed and closed his eyes.

Another day, another death.

Yes, it was a crucial role. He understood that. Countless directors had explained it to him. His dying was the catalyst for the human protagonist's growth, the loss that forces the hero to find the courage inside themself. The movie wouldn't work without that first poignant sacrifice that clinched the audience's emotional involvement. He had to be that sacrifice.

That didn't mean he wasn't sick and tired of it.

The trailer door burst open and there was Lou, big earrings jangling. Her poofy platinum-blond wig looked even more dishevelled than usual. She could barely fit into his small dog-accommodating trailer, a peeve she often groused about, but today it didn't seem to bother her.

Honey! she shouted. Good thing you're lying down. I have news. Big news.

Wolf barely raised his head. This was Lou all over. Getting hyped about another supporting—and dying—role in some cheap knock-off of something that another movie had already done, and better.

I know it's been getting to you, Lou said, the way they're always bumping you off in these flicks. Well, we can kiss those days goodbye. You've just been offered a really juicy part. I mean it. Star billing. It's the lead's beloved companion, who—

Wolf's head drooped.

No, wait, just listen, baby. It's big-budget, major studio. The star of *Eat, Shop, Die*, who's absolutely red-hot right now, has signed on. And here's the kicker. Your character doesn't bite it in the first reel.

Wolf's head came up again. His tail thumped against the trailer's vinyl floor.

Audiences are tired of seeing dogs die a gory death, Lou said. People won't even go to a movie anymore if they think the dog is going to snuff it halfway through. You can shoot, impale, eviscerate, and blow up all the human beings you like, no one bats an eye. But for God's sake, don't hurt the dog. That's too painful. Too real.

Wolf whined softly. This was what he'd worked for and dreamed of all these years. But it would mean he'd have to carry so much more of the story on his shoulders. He felt a roiling in his gut and wondered if he was ready.

No more buying the farm in scene one, Lou said. Isn't that great?

Wolf's ears twitched. There was something in her tone . . .

There's just one minor detail, Lou said.

Wolf cocked his head.

The script does call for you to die. Of cancer. But it's tastefully handled and it's at the end.

Wolf choked back a howl that came out as an undignified squeal.

At the *very* end, honey, Lou said. The big heart-wrenching finish. Trust me, this is a giant step forward. It really is. Have I ever steered you wrong? This is the big ticket at last. Sweetheart, you're gonna be a star.

You're sure about this? Lou whispered.

They were lounging in deck chairs beside the pool behind Wolf's impeccably restored art deco bungalow in the hills. Lou had recently quit smoking for the tenth time, but here she was indulging in a cigarette. Nearby, sipping an appletini and absently toeing the crystalline water, stood the up-and-coming young writer-director who had brought Wolf a script that producers were sure to sit up and beg for.

Wolf didn't reply. He wondered if he had moved beyond Lou, with her gaudy jewellery and fake hair. Maybe it was time to find a new agent, a younger one with a little more daring and imagination. Something to ponder, anyhow. What really mattered was that, after the runaway success of his first starring role as the Hero's Best Pal Who Dies of Cancer at the End, he had the clout to choose any project he pleased. And he had chosen.

I just don't know if people are ready for something like this, babe, Lou said. It's so . . . radical.

Yes, it is, the writer-director said, turning to face them. Radical. That's exactly what makes it worth doing.

No, dear, Lou said with a condescending smile. Money is what makes it worth doing.

Oh yes, money, the writer-director said. Money, money, money. Have you ever given a thought to the struggles that dogs and other animal actors have gone through to get taken seriously in this business? To be given the opportunities that human actors simply take for granted?

Of course I have, Lou said, stubbing out her cigarette in the ashtray on the glass side table. I've been struggling along with them.

Ah, right, your struggles. Tell us again how much trouble

you've had with the plumbing in your restored eighteenth-century manor house in the south of France.

Lou sat up, glaring.

Who's the one who discovered our mutual friend here, she shot back, when he was playing Angel Dog Number Three in some sappy Christmas twaddle for preschoolers? Who landed him his first decent gig as the adorable family mutt in those ads for life insurance? Who's stuck by him all these years, making sure he got his shots and deworming and made it to his therapy appointments on time and—

No one's questioning your commitment, the writer-director said. Just the limits of your vision.

My *vision*? What's that supposed to mean? My vision is fine. My vision is what paid for this house and this pool and that fancy drink in your hand, missy.

Missy? Oh wow. Take it easy, grandma, before you blow a gasket.

And you show some respect, brat. I was putting pups on the cover of *Variety* when you were still in diapers.

How fitting. Soon I'll be on the cover of *Variety* and you'll be the one in a diaper.

As the two of them went at it, Wolf climbed off his lounger and padded toward the open patio door. Let them lock horns. He knew he would get his way in the end. And anyhow, there was a bevy of eager young canine hopefuls inside, superfine bitches all, sleeping off last night's bacchanal. Perhaps one of them would join him for an afternoon romp in the hills.

Gone to the Dogs

In the history of cinema there are films that push boundaries and change the game. Then there's Unleashed, *a movie that boldly goes where no dog has gone before. Probably for a good reason.*

Produced by and starring Hollywood's superstar canine actor, Unleashed *opens with promise. We're introduced to a crew*

of scientists aboard the research starship Beagle II, *searching for signs of alien life in the cosmos. And they've brought a dog with them, a handsome fellow named, unsurprisingly, Darwin.*

Just as we're getting to know our protagonists, disaster strikes. After a catastrophic malfunction forces an evacuation of the ship, the crew's escape pod crashes on an unknown world. It's here that the film makes its bold move. The pod slams into the ground. There's a moment of silence, then movement. We expect to see at least some of the human crew emerging, battered but alive. Instead, Darwin crawls alone from the wreckage. The camera pans across the pod's interior, revealing the broken, lifeless bodies of the human crew.

Every. Single. One.

From this point, eight minutes into its two-and-a-half-hour run time, Unleashed *becomes* The Darwin Show, *for better or worse. Mostly worse.*

The film's ambition is clear: to tell a story entirely about a dog, sans humans. It's a radical departure from convention that sounds intriguing on paper. In execution, it turns out to be an endurance test that might well try the patience of even the most committed dog-loving moviegoer.

Reliant on humans for everything until now, Darwin must quickly learn how to survive. He finds food (only some of it edible) and narrowly avoids rockfalls and poisonous stinging plants. The film injects some drama with the introduction of a malevolent alien presence that stalks Darwin through the underbrush, but without human reaction or dialogue to contextualize the threat, these scenes fall flat. The unfortunate overuse of a jerky dog's-eye-view camera angle left me queasy. Darwin's reactions—alternating between growls and yips—convey very little when you don't speak dog. If you thought Keanu had a limited range, well, whoa.

Midway through the film we're introduced to a potential love interest: Astra, a fellow canine survivor from an earlier *crashed space mission. She's been waiting here years for rescue, but it appears she may also be keeping a secret from our furry hero. Here's a chance for the action to really take off, but instead we're treated to a long sequence of what I could only assume was meant to be flirtatious butt-sniffing. Astra and Darwin's inevitable showdown with the aliens (who fittingly resemble giant cats) could have been thrilling, but lacking human actors as our emotional surrogates, it felt somehow inconsequential. There's no tearful reunion with a loving owner at the end of this incredible journey. It's dogs all the way down.*

There's an argument to be made for Unleashed *as a story that challenges our supposed supremacy as a species and invites us to engage with a truly different perspective.*

If only the movie wasn't as boring as a dog's ass.

Perhaps the most telling criticism came from the kid sitting behind me at the screening. About an hour in she loudly asked, "Mommy, when are the people coming back?" I'd been wondering the same thing.

1½ paws out of five

Scene one, the clapper loader said. Take seven.

Roll it, the AD said. Cue the dog.

So here he was again.

The trainer touched Wolf's flank and off he went, dashing across a stretch of bright green artificial turf into the waiting arms of a laughing child and a smiling senior citizen. The finished commercial for bran flakes, he knew, would show the sequence in slow motion, through a gauzy filter that would make everything warm and sunny and nostalgic.

Cut, the AD said.

Lou had dumped him as a client and the writer-director wasn't returning his calls. From the dizzying heights he'd tumbled back down to the mean streets, his career a poop bag

squashed under a car tire. And to top it all off, he was pretty sure he had dysplasia, or maybe some kind of tumour festering in his left hip. He'd been hiding it, biting back cries of pain. Once they noticed, it was all over. You never got another chance in this human-eat-dog town.

Not sure what's up with the dog, the AD said after reviewing the take. Let's break for twenty. And somebody find the vet.

Wolf limped back to his kennel, hip throbbing in agony, and flopped down on the thin rubber mat. The vet would come and look him over, prod him and palpate him, and he'd be finished. Tossed out. Maybe even put down. He should just die right now and get it over with. Would it matter to anyone if he never got up again?

He let out a long sigh.

Roscoe? said a voice. Wolf raised his head. His heart began to hammer. A boy stood in front of the kennel, tears brimming in his eyes.

It had been such a long road, but Wolf knew him right away. How could he ever forget? It was Cody. His first friend. His best friend.

His boy.

Oh, Roscoe, Cody said. I thought I'd never see you again. What have they done to you?

Wolf rose unsteadily to his feet and limped into Cody's arms. Oh, how he had longed to feel these arms and hear that voice, if only one last time. Together. They were together again. A boy and his dog. Until death, whenever that came and parted them.

And *cut*, the director said.

Okay, get off me, said the actor playing Cody. You need a bath.

That's a wrap, people, the director said. Nice work. *A Dog's Life* is in the can.

Park

Wolf was just over a year old and prone to the zoomies. A brisk walk around the block wasn't enough to tire him out anymore, so the man brought him to a dog park.

Here we are, the man said, and sighed. Let's see how this goes.

Wolf hadn't socialized much with other dogs and was timid around his own kind. At the gate he tried to back away.

Come on, the man said, tugging on the leash. It's for your own good.

When he'd managed to haul Wolf inside, the man sat down on the nearest bench and unclipped his leash.

Go on, he said.

Wolf stood there, anxiously glancing this way and that.

It was a big park, with lots of space to roam. But there were so many dogs here. Big dogs, smaller dogs, freakishly tiny things that were somehow still dogs. Dogs with fancy collars. Dogs with odd haircuts and perfumed fur. Dogs whose owners kept them on a tight leash and dogs who'd left their owners far behind the minute they came through the gate.

Wolf looked up at the man. The man looked at Wolf.

Go on, go, the man said. You can run your ass off here. Seriously. It's okay.

Wolf trotted half-heartedly away, glancing back often at the bench and the man.

Go, the man said, waving an impatient hand.

Wolf approached a miniature poodle who looked friendly. The poodle's owner scooped up the poodle and told Wolf to shoo.

The man was looking at his phone and didn't notice.

Wolf sniffed a patch of clover. He peed on it, glancing back at the bench. The man looked up from his phone and gave Wolf a thumbs-up.

First time here? someone asked.

The man looked up to see an old guy in a thick down jacket that was too heavy for the warm weather. The old man sat down beside him on the bench. He didn't appear to have a dog with him. In his hand was a plastic shopping bag that looked weighed down with something heavy. He set the bag at his feet.

Yep, first time, the man said. How could you tell?

I've been coming here a long time. I can always tell. I'm willing to bet he's not your dog either.

That's right, the man said. He's my daughter's.

Nice of you to look after him.

Didn't really have a choice. She just had a baby and this guy didn't take well to the new addition.

That happens sometimes. They usually get over it.

Yeah, I know. But my daughter didn't want to take any chances, so I've got him until we can find him a new home.

The two men sat there. They watched dogs come and go. Neither of them said anything for a while.

I'm Jerry, the old man finally said.

Hi, the man said. He didn't offer his own name.

You want a beer? Jerry asked.

It's ten in the morning.
It's light beer.
The man thought about it.
Sure, he said.
Jerry took two cans of beer out of the bag. He gave one to the man, who pulled the tab and took a sip.
Wolf trotted up to a tall, slender greyhound being walked by a frail-looking older woman. Wolf followed them, sniffing at the greyhound's butt. The greyhound ignored Wolf and kept walking.
The old woman noticed Wolf trailing them.
Go on, get out of here, she said sharply, looking around for Wolf's owner. Wolf trotted back in the direction of the bench.
Funny, Jerry said. How they don't care.
Who? the man asked.
The dogs. They couldn't care less about breed and all that shit. To them a butt is a butt. A dog is a dog. But people, they look at a dog like yours and figure it's got to be dangerous.
I've noticed, the man said.
As he neared the bench, Wolf crossed paths with a small white-and-tan terrier. They made playful bows at each other and then tumbled together. Wolf pinned the terrier on its back and it gave a yelp.
A young woman came running up, screaming, Precious!
Wolf shied away in fear. The woman picked up her trembling terrier.
Is this your dog? she said to the man.
It is, the man said.
What's wrong with you? she said over her shoulder as she walked away. If he doesn't know how to behave in a dog park, keep him on a leash.
They were just playing, the man said.
Drinking isn't allowed in the park either, the young woman said. I should report you two.

Go ahead, said Jerry. That would make your day, wouldn't it?

The young woman didn't answer. She hurried away, glancing over her shoulder to see if Wolf was following. The terrier was wagging its tail. Wolf loped after them, as if there was a chance for more play.

Dog, the man said to Wolf. Come here.

Wolf came back, panting happily.

Maybe I should do as she said and put this leash on you, the man said. I don't really want to, though.

He clipped the leash onto Wolf's collar.

You just call him Dog? Jerry asked.

He's got a name, the man said. It's just not a name people like to hear. They think he's dangerous enough already.

Jerry sipped his beer and contemplated.

Fang? he asked.

No.

Mugsy. Killer.

No.

Let's see. Adolph.

Are you kidding me?

Yeah, not likely. Hitler did have a dog, though. Its name was Blondi. A German shepherd, big surprise. Shepherds were like the master race of dog breeds over there. Because they look like wolves, right? Hitler really loved dogs. In the bunker, when Blondi was put down so she wouldn't get captured by the Soviets, he completely lost it.

Where's your dog? the man asked.

It's just me, Jerry said. I like it here in the mornings. Watching the dogs. Don't have much to do now that I'm retired.

Why not get a dog then?

I had one.

Jerry finished his beer, crushed the can, and dropped it back into the bag.

Care for another? he asked the man.

No, thanks. We should probably get going.
Do you mind if I tell this guy a story first? Jerry asked.
You want to tell the dog a story?
It's about a dog. The pup might find it interesting.
The man shrugged.
I guess. Go ahead.
Addressing Wolf, Jerry began, Once upon a time, there was this dog from what they called the wrong side of the tracks. People took one look at him and decided he was no good. And everything he did, it was like he set out to prove them right. You know what, let's call him Jimmy.
Jerry laughed.
Yeah, Jimmy, that was the dog's name. Jimmy got into a lot of fights and stole things and just generally ran wild, and finally the law caught up with him. He got six months in the pound and let me tell you, it scared him but good. When he got out he swore he was gonna be a new dog. So he went out and got a decent-paying job and worked hard and didn't get into any trouble.
Jerry paused. When he spoke next his voice was quieter.
One night Jimmy met this girl dog, at a doggy dance.
A doggy dance, the man said. Okay.
Let's call her Abby, since that was her name. Abby was quiet, sensible, a real good girl—everything Jimmy wasn't. Well, he fell for her like a ton of bricks. After a few weeks of dating they skipped the engagement and eloped. They bought a little doghouse and had two sweet little puppies, a boy and a girl, and life was good.
That's nice. Well—
Hang on, there's more. Because life was good, of course Jimmy had to go and screw it all up. Didn't he, pup? Yes, he did. Some of his buddies from his wild days found him, or he found them, and he started hanging around with them again and leaving Abby at home with the pups. One night at a bar he met this waitress, this foxy little bitch who was nothing but

trouble. Anyone with half a brain could see it, but Jimmy wasn't too bright about things like that. So Jimmy hooked up with her, not knowing she already had a boyfriend. Anyhow, Jimmy and the boyfriend found out about each other, and they got into a fight and the boyfriend ended up with permanent brain damage and couldn't feed himself anymore. The animal control judge sentenced Jimmy to twelve years for aggravated assault.

Wolf sighed and stretched out at Jerry's feet. Jerry laughed softly.

It's okay, pup, he said. We're just coming to the good part. When Jimmy got out, well, guess what, he was an old dog. Abby had divorced him while he was inside and moved across the country, and their puppies had grown up and as far as he knew they didn't want nothing to do with him. He didn't even know where they lived or what they looked like anymore. So our boy Jimmy got a job and went to work and ate and slept. That was his life. That was it.

Jerry sat up straight, waiting until Wolf met his gaze.

And that, he said, is when the dog showed up.

Wolf cocked his head, wary now.

I thought Jimmy was the dog, the man said.

Jimmy was a dog who decided to get himself a dog. That's the story.

All right, fine.

It was a rescue dog that had been abused something awful. The dog's name was Orville.

Listen—

See, Jimmy had been keeping to himself—it was safer that way—but he was lonely, so he got the dog. They went everywhere together. They went fishing and duck hunting and just wandering around, seeing the sights. One time they took a trip to the badlands and scrambled around the hoodoos and waded barefoot in the river. Orville found a bone in the water, a long bone like a propeller blade with a hole in one end. This park interpreter fellow told Jimmy it was from a bison's hump and it had probably been lying on that riverbed for maybe five hundred years. Imagine that. Long before any of us palefaces came along. Jimmy was going to take his find home and display it on a shelf. It was a keepsake. Then, later, at the campsite, he cocked back his arm and threw the bone far out into the river. Splash. *Bye-bye, buffalo,* he shouted, and then he laughed. Jimmy just did things sometimes for no good reason. And Orville, he just sat there, he didn't bother to chase after the bone, like Jimmy taking away his big find was just the latest disappointment in life.

A car door slammed. The man looked at the fence and saw a cop walking toward the gate.

That'll be for me, Jerry said.

He picked up his shopping bag and stood.

Nice meeting you, he said to the man, then turned to Wolf. You too, pup, he said.

His name's Wolf, the man said.

Wolf, Jerry said. It suits him.

The cop was at the gate now, talking to the young woman with the terrier, who turned and pointed at Jerry.

What about the dog? the man asked.

What's that? Jerry asked.

The dog. Orville.

Right. Orville.

The cop was walking toward them now across the grass.

Orville wasn't a bad dog deep down, but he was never right in the head after all that had happened to him. He got really aggressive with other dogs. Finally, one day he attacked a neighbour's puppy and killed it, and Jimmy, well, he did what had to be done. Once a dog's crossed that line, that's who it'll be forever.

Jerry leaned down and scratched Wolf between the ears.

And that's it, pup, he said. That's all she wrote. The moral of the story is, be a good dog. Remember that.

The cop was big and frowning, and he had shades on. He slowed up when he got to the bench.

Jerry, he said. I've told you. Haven't I told you?

Yeah, you have, Jerry said. Here.

He handed the cop his shopping bag.

After you, the cop said.

Jerry started walking toward the gate and the cop followed.

Wolf and the man watched them go.

Moondog

This is Comet. He's a very special dog.
Comet is the first dog to live on the Moon.

Comet was chosen from dozens of puppies.
His puppy name was Wolf.
He was so bright and quick, everyone called him Comet.

Doctor Chandra is Comet's trainer and best friend.
She trained Comet for his important job.

He floated in a pool and spun in a big machine.
This helped him get ready for living and working in space.

One day Comet was finally ready to go. He was so excited!
Comet and Doctor Chandra climbed aboard the shuttle.
With a roar it flew up into the sky.

The shuttle travelled through space for three days.
Comet saw the Earth from space.
It looked like a blue marble that got smaller and smaller.

The shuttle landed at Hypatia Colony, near the Moon's south pole.
Comet was on the Moon at last!

Everything was new and strange.
Comet could jump really high because the Moon has less gravity than Earth.
This makes everything lighter, even a dog.

The people who live at the colony were happy to meet Comet.
They gave him lots of hugs and cuddles.

Comet expected to find the Great Mother waiting for him.
She wasn't there.
But the Moon was a big place.
Much bigger than it looked from Earth.
Maybe the Great Mother lived somewhere else on the Moon.
Maybe She would come visit him one day.
He would wait.

There's no need to howl at the Moon when you're on it.

Here's a photograph of Comet with the colonists.
Comet has an important job to do on the Moon.
When the colonists miss their families back on Earth, Comet cheers them up.

Comet spends time with everyone at the colony.
He's good at his job and he really loves it.

Comet plays fetch with the colonists.
The ball goes really far in Moon gravity.

Comet can't go outside, but he has a special room to play in.
It has dirt and grass, and bones to find and bury.
The room plays the sounds of birds and running water and wind.

The dirt in the room has a funny smell that Comet doesn't like.
A smell that tells Comet it isn't real dirt.
Just like the bones aren't real bones.
The dirt is *clean* dirt.
It will have to do.

Sometimes Comet finds a colonist in his room.
Sometimes the colonist just sits in the grass.
Sometimes they smear dirt on themselves and weep.
Comet's job is to help humans live on the Moon.
He sits with the colonist until they feel better.

On a wall at the colony there's a picture of a dog.
It's Laika, the first dog to orbit the Earth.
Doctor Chandra tells Comet how important Laika was to humans.
She doesn't say what happened to her after she went up into space.
Why isn't she here for Comet to meet?
When his work is done will he disappear too?

At night Comet looks out the window at the Earth.
He thinks about the other dogs he knew.
Comet has boldly gone where no dog has gone before.
Sometimes it's lonely being the first.

There is no night at Hypatia Colony.
It's always daytime here.
The colonists make a pretend nighttime by turning off lights.
This helps Comet get to sleep.

Good night, Moon.
Good night, Earth.
Good night, Comet.
Sweet dreams, first dog on the Moon.

Laika

Stage Two

A voice spoke from nowhere.
Woof.
Wolf opened her eyes.

She was no longer in the capsule. She was in a warm, quiet room, lying on a soft bed. Her flight suit was gone and there were tubes and wires attached to her body. She was groggy and her eyes couldn't quite focus yet, but she was aware of banks of lights above her, fuzzy ovals of pale gold. She blinked and strained her eyes to see better. The walls of this place were curved and looked to be made of something soft, not at all like the room of cages she'd lived in before.

This was nowhere she had ever been.

Wolf felt a jolt of fear, but then noticed there was a smell in the air she remembered, and it calmed her. It was the scent of everything the cold in the capsule had taken from her.

Life.

Someone stood at her side. She turned her head.

It was another dog. A big black dog with a friendly face.

Woof huffa wuff, said the dog.

Wolf raised her head, trying to reach the other dog's snout to lick it. This dog wasn't going to attack her, she understood, but she was weak and defenceless and she had to make sure it understood she was no threat.

Hoofa huff wowshuff wuff, said the big black dog. Then he reached out a paw and touched something that had been placed on Wolf's forehead. A small, scentless thing that gave off a low hum.

There, said the dog. That should help. Can you understand me now?

Yes, said Wolf, startled to hear herself answer. New things were flooding into her head. Pictures of things she knew.

Good, said the dog. His voice was deep and warm and even soothing. My name is Skylos. I'm so glad to meet you. What should I call you?

The question made Wolf's heart throb with longing for someone she couldn't bring to mind. Someone long gone.

I don't know, she said. They gave me so many names. Little Bug, that was one. And Curly, and Barker . . .

She hesitated. It was almost as if she could hear their voices calling her from an immense distance.

That's all right, Skylos said softly. Here you don't have to have a name if you don't want one.

Here. What . . . (*more things and more words jumping together*) . . . where are we?

A safe place, Skylos said. There's much to tell you, but what's most important right now is that you rest. Rest and heal. There will be plenty of time later for talk.

Skylos gently patted Wolf's head. As Wolf sank back down

into a warm sleep, it occurred to her that where Skylos's dewclaw should have been, the big dog had a thumb.

When Wolf woke, Skylos was there at her side, along with a smaller grey dog who also had thumbs on her front paws. Wolf thought it better not to mention this in case it was some kind of deformity.

Hello, I'm Bau, said the new dog. How are you feeling?

Hungry, Wolf said.

Bau laughed, a sound Wolf had never heard a dog make before. The hair rose on her neck.

I'm sure you are, Bau said. I think you're well enough to get up and have a meal.

Wolf climbed from the bed. As her paws met the strange springiness of the floor, a stab of fear shot through her, but she did her best not to show it.

Then she smelled the gleaming cube of meat on a low wooden table nearby. Wolf padded over and devoured it in three bites. It was good, it was fresh raw meat, but there was something more, or not more, *less*—a missing something she hadn't noticed before in any food she'd ever eaten, because it had always been there.

Good, said Bau. You have a healthy appetite.

What is this? Wolf asked. It's not pig. Or cow.

Forgive me, Bau said. I forgot that where you're from the meat came from killing other animals. We grow ours in our labs, to produce the maximum nutritional benefits and extend our canine lifespans, which are still regrettably short. Although we have pushed back our expiry date quite a bit since your day.

You . . . *grow* meat? Wolf asked. She remembered the fields of grain that the humans tended all summer and harvested when the weather turned. How she'd chased rats sometimes in those fields before she came to the city, where there were even more rats.

Yes, said Bau. Well, I don't, not personally. I'm a healer. I was one of those who helped bring you back from the void. You were gone and we thought we were too late, but you came back. It was your own fighting spirit more than anything we did. You so wanted to live. As for Skylos here, he is what we call a cynonaut. He's the one who found you and rescued you from the capsule before the heat finished you.

Where am I? Wolf asked.

Welcome, Skylos said in his deep, reassuring voice, to the Planet of Dogs.

The Planet of Dogs. After hearing that such a place existed and she was there, Wolf found it hard to rest. Bau came to see her every day and asked her about what she remembered from before and what she had learned since waking up. He showed Wolf images on a glowing screen and asked her to connect the images with one another. Wolf learned about the picture things in her head that she now understood were called ideas, which she could nose together with other ideas to make more ideas. It was like the training the humans had put her through, only for her mind rather than her body.

When she wasn't making new idea-pictures she mostly rested.

Then one day Bau announced that she was recovered enough, and had learned enough, to go outside.

Skylos came and led her down a long hallway and out a door that slid open like an eye. Wolf's own eyes blinked in the sudden glare of sunlight. Among the new pictures she had in her head now was how that blazing ball up there was one of those icy specks in the blackness called stars, only much closer. How there were other planets flying like birds around other stars in space. And space was where she had gone in the capsule. The thought made her head spin, and she cowered and backed into Skylos.

It's all right, he said. Take your time.

The building she had been in, Wolf could see now, was a large dome covered in lush grass. Outside its doors so many familiar scents, sounds, and sights came all at once they nearly overwhelmed her senses, but the big black dog was beside her and she mastered her fear and began to look around.

Before them lay an open field of grass and flowers with trees at its edges. In the midst of it was a still pond fringed with reeds. And there were dogs everywhere. So many dogs. Some were running. Some were play-fighting. Some were digging holes to bury bones. Some were lying in the grass just soaking up the sun.

The funny thing was, all the dogs looked much like Skylos and Bau. They were different sizes and their coats were different colours, but they all had long snouts and big paws and pointy, upright ears. What was this? Were they all one big family?

Then Wolf was distracted by other things she hadn't seen in so long. Birds chirping and flitting in the trees. Squirrels racing up and down branches. Bees humming in the flowers.

And the air. The air was clean. So clean. There was no trace of the stinging particles and fumes she had known in her life with humans.

Wolf's tail began to wag.

Yes, said Skylos. It's a most dogulent thing, isn't it.

Wolf walked with Skylos through the field. A few dogs came trotting over and gathered around her in a friendly manner. They said things like *Welcome home* and *We're so glad you made it*.

Wolf shrank from them. They were dogs, but not at all like the dogs she had known before she went up in the capsule. They didn't sniff her anus or display dominance or submissiveness, or do anything else she might have expected from dogs she'd never met.

They know who I am? Wolf asked when the dogs had trotted calmly away.

They do indeed. We all do. You're famous.

Famous?

A legend.

These were new words, new ideas. Wolf asked Skylos to explain.

Well, a legend is someone who does what no one else dared to do. They go where others fear to go, and it changes things forever.

I see, Wolf said. I think. What did I do that made me a legend?

The humans who sent you above the Earth in that little tin pet carrier, Skylos said. Do you know why they did it?

I saw a big blue ball when I was up there, Wolf said. I didn't know it was the Earth. I thought they wanted me to chase it.

Skylos laughed. Wolf still wasn't used to this human sound coming from a dog, but Skylos's laugh was so warm and friendly it had to be all right.

My friend, you are without a doubt the most doggish dog I've ever met, he said. And I mean that as the sincerest compliment. No, they sent you up to circle the planet simply to see if it could be done. No animal had gone on that journey before. You were the very first. I wonder, did you ask yourself why they sent you, a dog, instead of one of their own kind?

No.

It was because they knew you wouldn't be coming back. They sent you up to travel around the Earth, but in those primitive days they had no way to bring you down safely. They sent you up there knowing you would die.

But they were kind to me. They gave me food and a safe place to sleep. The boss human took me home, to play with his children. They . . . loved me.

Yes. I'm sure they did, in their way. I don't doubt that the humans regretted what they felt they had to do. But they believed their own kind was more important than dog kind. If they were going to send one of their own up, they needed to know what would happen first. That's why they chose you.

I understand. No, I don't. Not really. Why did they want to know if it could be done? Why didn't they want to stay on Earth? There's nothing up there but cold and dark.

She shivered at the memory.

The humans were in a kind of race with one another, Skylos said. There were two big powerful packs at that time, and each struggled to dominate the other. They both wanted to be the first to do astonishing new things, like sending an animal into orbit. They thought that would show all the humans which pack was the strongest and the best.

So I was supposed to die.

Yes. They considered it a regrettable but necessary side effect of the experiment. But what they could never have imagined was just how much further you would travel. You left them far behind.

I left the Earth?

You could say that, yes. It's hard to explain, I'm afraid. It will take time before you can put these ideas together in a way that will make sense to you. All I will say for now is that this is no longer your Earth. You've travelled to another one.

Another . . . planet.

Wolf searched and found one of the new thoughts that had flooded into her head.

That sun up there . . . she said breathlessly, unable to form the words she needed. More strange thoughts tumbled past and she nosed them together into a new shape.

You have thumbs, she said. You don't act like the dogs I knew.

Her tail wagged. In her excitement she spun in a circle and jumped. This was a whole new world to explore. She pointed her nose at the blazing light high above.

That's Sirius, the dog star, isn't it? she said. This really *is* the Planet of Dogs.

Skylos didn't answer. He looked at Wolf with something like awe.

I'm beginning to see why the humans chose you, my friend, he said. You're ready for pretty much anything. No, you didn't travel quite that far, I'm afraid. Or not in that way. But let's go back now. Bau insists we take things one step at a time. Besides, we've put together something special for you this evening, so you'll want to be good and rested up.

At sunset Skylos invited Wolf to go out into the field.

The great space was lit with hovering globes of warm light. Many dogs were gathered there, around a large, circular open space.

Skylos showed Wolf to a place at the edge of the circle. She watched, bewildered, as a group of dogs walked solemnly into the middle of the empty grass ring.

A hush fell among the watching crowd. One of the dogs, wearing a kind of vest and leggings, rose up on its hind legs. It swayed awkwardly at first, but then it steadied itself and stood fully upright—like a human, Wolf realized in shock. The human-like dog held its nose high and gazed impassively at the other dogs, who began to fall into line around it, plodding snout to tail with one another, around and around, like a circle within the circle. Then the human dog raised one of its front paws. The others all stopped. They turned toward the human dog and lowered their heads and tails. Then the human dog lowered its paw, and the dogs resumed their plodding orbit.

Another dog, a small one, ran out of the crowd. It wore a strange transparent bubble on its head, and its body was sheathed in shiny silver fabric. This dog cut through the circling dogs to the far side of the ring and back, again and again.

Then more dogs darted in to join whatever this was. They carried long, ragged pieces of fabric in their mouths, in shades of yellow, brown, and grey, and some, longer and more billowy than the others, that were a bright and shiny blue. These dogs broke apart the ring of circling dogs and soon all was chaos, with dogs lunging, spinning, bounding, jumping. The human dog in the middle fell out of sight.

Then somehow this confusion resolved itself, and Wolf saw that the dogs were moving in a kind of harmony, like the planets and stars. They wove around one another, forming pairs and triplets and little gangs, until it became clear to Wolf that they were all one pack with no leaders and no followers, only companions. The colours merged and parted and merged again. The little dog with the bubble on its head, running far out on its lone trajectory, was found by others among the pack and brought among them. The human dog, it seemed, was gone, or it had become one of the others.

Then the dogs ceased their antics, and all those gathered to watch them burst into a wild, joyful clamour of barking. Wolf shrank down in alarm, but Skylos nudged up against her gently and said it was all right. There was no threat to her here and there never would be. Still Wolf cowered. What did it all mean? It had frightened her and for some reason made her sad, but the dogs near her in the crowd were looking at her eagerly, as if expecting her to bark joyously too. It seemed this had all been for her, whatever it was.

She was surrounded by her own kind, and she was alone.

The next morning Bau came to examine Wolf. He seemed satisfied with what he found, and gave his approval for Wolf to begin the next phase of her recovery.

Skylos led her from the room. She had been eager to leave before, but now she felt a chill of unease. What else was coming that she wouldn't understand?

This time they walked all the way to the far end of the big field and kept going, crossing over a stream on a fallen tree. On the far side they took a rough path lined with bushes that Wolf's

nose told her innumerable others had peed on. The thought cheered her a little, but she tired quickly and Skylos stopped so she could rest a while in the cool shade, with the richly scented breeze stirring her coat. When they moved on again Wolf began to catch another scent, one that was in her ears and in her paws and fur all at the same time, a smell that was a sound that was an itch. It was very strange. Her hackles rose.

They came to a kind of wall that gleamed like water and reflected the trees, the sky, and Wolf back to herself. She was about to bark at that other dog intently gazing back at her, but in a flash she understood who it was.

Skylos stopped.

This may be difficult for you, he said. Maybe we should come back another day, when you've had more time to get used to things. I don't want to upset you, my friend.

Upset me? What is it?

This is a fence in front of us. It keeps us dogs safe and keeps . . . the others out.

Others. What others?

The ones we can't have on this side. Not yet.

A pang stabbed Wolf's heart. Like a faint echo in her ears came the howling she'd heard at night from the dark, snow-shrouded plains beyond the launch site.

Wolves, she breathed. Are there wolves out there? I want to see them. Please, Skylos. Let me see them.

They're not wolves, Skylos said. We're the wolves now.

How can that be?

The only way to save the wolf was to backbreed it with the dog. Bau and I and the others, we're the descendants of that reunion. It gave our species the one trait of the wolf we dogs had lost that we'd need to survive: the ability to work together to solve problems.

But I heard them on the steppe, before I left. That was only days ago. What happened to them?

Skylos gazed at her for a long moment. Then he sighed.

Bau feels we should wait, but I disagree. You deserve to know. You must've wondered why we all look so much alike.

I did. And also why—why there are no humans.

Skylos's soft laugh sounded somehow sad.

I guess this is my big Toto moment, he said.

Skylos raised his thumbed paw and Wolf saw that a small metal device was strapped to his ankle (which was also his wrist). Skylos spoke into the device.

Raise the security curtain, he said. Sector K Eleven.

The water wall began to ripple, sending shards of flashing sunlight into Wolf's eyes so that she blinked and jumped back.

Then the strange water was gone and Wolf could see what she had caught the scent of.

There they are, Skylos said.

Wolf looked. They were wearing rough skins for clothing. Some were digging for roots in the earth. Others were chipping at stones with other stones. When they engaged with one another they grunted and gestured.

One of them noticed the window. It came loping over, hunched, wary, sniffing. When it got close it suddenly lunged forward and hammered the invisible barrier with its fists. It shouted—words, perhaps, or just noises. Wolf couldn't hear anything through the wall. The others noticed and came hurrying over. They pounded and clawed at the wall too, their mouths agape with silent screams.

Wolf turned to Skylos with an anguished moan.

Lower the curtain, the big dog said into his device. The maddened humans vanished and the water returned.

What . . . what happened to them? Wolf asked, shaken. The ones I knew weren't like *this*.

No. Not the ones you knew. That was a long time ago. They were strong then, and smarter, or at least cunning in a primate sort of way. But they were not wise. They fought each other for dominance, they retreated into packs and kept up hostilities when they should have worked together. As time ran out to repair the damage they'd done to the planet, they retreated into themselves, into imaginary lives served up to them by their devices. While they were looking away, the wolves edged to the brink of vanishing, and many other living things with them.

Wolf's insides went cold.

How could all this have happened so quickly?

It took many lifetimes. Your rocket made its flight thousands of years ago, my friend.

Thousands. But that's impossible. I can't be that old.

You aren't. You're not much more than two. Through the ages, we'd kept your story alive as part of our history. We've always thought of you as the first of us—the first dog to point the way to the future. That's why we so longed to meet you. When our technology advanced to the point where we could bring you here, to us, we made it happen. You could say we dug a hole through time to find you. We were able to rescue you from the capsule once your movement and blood pressure monitors had overheated and failed and the humans on the ground had lost your signal. At that point they had no way of knowing what was happening to you. We brought you here, to our time, back through the hole we'd dug. The humans who sent you into space believed you'd burned up with the rocket on re-entry and your atoms were scattered through the atmosphere. Because you were so far above the planet and your fate was already sealed, we knew we could remove you from the timestream without fear of altering vital events on Earth.

Wait. No. You're saying this is—she groped for the word that went with the idea—the future?

Actually, this is *now*. I know it's difficult, my friend. Your time was the distant past. Immense changes have occurred since your rocket left Earth. The humans wounded the planet so grievously that many of them perished as well. Some left in great vessels the size of cities, to search among the stars for a new home. Those who remained on Earth took refuge in shelters underground and in time became all but merged with their devices. They tried to control things from there.

But these ones here—they're not under the ground.

Not anymore. It's a long story. To tell it properly one has to go back to the beginning, really. Dogs and humans created one another, did you know that? We wouldn't have existed without them, and without us they would never have grown past what you see through that window. How strange that of all the creatures on Earth we chose each other, to weave our fates together. And yet, for a long time, one of us dominated the other. They made the rules and called the shots. A dog's purpose was to guard the camp. A dog's purpose was to herd the flocks. A dog's purpose was unquestioning obedience, faithful companionship, unconditional love. We gave them everything and they never stopped demanding more. As if we existed only for *them*, not for ourselves.

Wolf was surprised at the heat that had crept into Skylos's voice.

They taught us to fight in their wars, the big dog went on. To fly in their rockets. They enslaved us and experimented on us and turned us into freaks and mutants to suit their crazy whims. Over and over again, humans reinvented the dog, and the meaning of the dog, for themselves. In the end, to tend the world they had all but destroyed, the humans *improved* us one last time, to make us the stewards they had failed to be. These thumbs, you see? And the breeding for cooperation. While they flew away in their starships and hid underground in their virtual cocoons, we took on our oldest roles once more, in a new way. We became guardians and shepherds, not just of flocks this time, but of all life.

The air, Wolf said. The water. The grass. Birds. Bees. You fixed it. You fixed everything.

We did what was necessary and found ways to help the planet heal itself. And in doing that, this time we reinvented ourselves. Meanwhile the machines that kept the humans fed and comfortable underground began to fail. They had become so utterly dependent on them that when they were forced to leave them and return to the surface, they were all but helpless. They're having to learn everything they once knew, all over again.

You can help them, Wolf said in anguish. You have all these wondrous things. You taught me to understand your language in no time at all. You could do the same for them. Why don't you? They were kind to me. Some of them were. They can be good. They can be our friends again.

You and I are the same species. They are not. I know it seems cruel to keep them like this, but we've learned we must be so careful about what we teach them, and how. Every tool we've given them they have quickly put to harmful use. So we made the choice to keep them on a short leash for now, you might say, with only the most basic means to survive. There's too much to lose if we get this wrong. But Bau and the others who designed the rehabilitation program are hopeful. They believe that humans can learn, and change. They look forward to the day we may be companions again. One thing I know for certain, though. When that day comes, everything will be different.

Wolf and Skylos returned to the dome. Wolf went to her sleeping place and lay there, shifting restlessly, with all she had seen and experienced in the past few days racing through her mind.

Later, unable to fall asleep, she got up and went out to relieve herself. It was late afternoon and the sun was casting golden shafts of light through the trees. There were no dogs in the field.

Wolf did her business, but she didn't go back to the dome. Instead she kept walking until she reached the strange wall of water, with its itchy, tingling feeling that made her so uneasy.

She sat there in front of the wall, straining her nose and ears. She couldn't smell or hear anything, but she knew the humans were there, on the other side. What were they doing? Even though there were many of them, they were so alone.

The sun went down and a few stars began to twinkle in the darkening sky. The wind came up. It was getting cold. Still Wolf sat in front of the wall.

There you are, said a familiar voice. It was Skylos.

We were worried when you went out and didn't come back, he said. I figured I might find you here.

Wolf said nothing.

Just look at those stars tonight, Skylos said. So beautiful.

He lifted a paw.

You see those five stars up there? The humans called them the Big Dog. And those two there, above the Big Dog, the humans called them the Little Dog. We still call them that, but now we have our own names for all the others. If you look over there, you can see—

I can't stay, Wolf said. I can't stay here.

Skylos tilted his head in surprise.

But you can't go back. It's not possible.

That's not what I mean. I can't stay here with *you*. With the others.

I know it must all seem so strange, but if you just give it some time, give *us* some time—

It wouldn't make any difference. I need to go . . . over there. With them.

Skylos gaped.

With the—? No. What? No, you can't mean that.

Why not?

You don't know these humans. They're not like the ones you lived with. You said so yourself.

Neither are you, or the other dogs.

But—no, it's not the same. Who knows what might happen to you in there. What those creatures are capable of. It's just not safe.

Right. Who knows what might happen. That's where I'm from, a place where you never know. That's where I belong. You said you're hoping to be friends with them again. Helping them find the way—that's something *I* can do.

The big dog wuffed angrily and pawed the ground.

No, he said. No, I can't allow it. I won't. I saved you, and my job now is to keep you from harm.

Then you'll be keeping me in a cage. Just like they did.

But . . . but . . . what they did to you? They don't deserve you!

Deserve. This was one of the ideas Wolf had yet to fully take in.

You know that, don't you? Skylos said. After all they've done to our kind, they don't deserve any of us.

You told me you think of me as the first, but I feel like the last, Wolf said. The last dog on Earth. And it's why I'm the one who can do this.

The big dog fumed. He paced back and forth, muttering, It's foolhardy. It's mad. It's incredibly dangerous.

It's something else, too, Wolf said. It's doggish.

Skylos stopped pacing. His eyes went so comically wide Wolf had to laugh. Her first laugh.

Skylos laughed too. He gazed at her a long time, then he sighed and nuzzled Wolf's snout with his own.

I don't want this for you, my friend, he said, and it saddens my heart. But you're right, I can't stop you. And maybe you are the only one who can attempt this. The one who can go where no one else has dared. Listen, though, will you stay one more night with us? So we can tell Bau and the others, and give you a proper farewell?

Yes, Wolf said. I can do that.

She and Skylos headed back the way they had come. When they were nearing the grassy dome a bright yellow moon peeked out over the tops of the trees, like an egg sitting atop a great nest.

There she is, Skylos said. Smiling down on us.

Can the humans see her, where they are? Wolf asked.

Only as a faint blur, I believe.

Can you change that? Can you give them a window where they can watch her?

I imagine we can. Hard to say what they'd think about her, though. Probably just one more thing out of their reach.

Yes. That's why they've always needed us.

WOLF

PART 2

Wolf followed the boy and his humans upriver, onto a rolling highland scoured by deep ravines. The air warmed and every day the sun climbed higher into the sky.

After many sleeps they came to a place where other humans, from many different packs, were camped. They greeted the new arrivals with smiles and handclasps, but when they set eyes on Wolf these new humans lost their minds, and once again the boy's father had to rush in and calm things down.

That night the newcomers joined the other humans around a big, blazing fire. Stories were shared, songs were sung, dances were danced. Some kind of unpleasant-smelling drink was passed around that made the humans laugh louder and dance even more foolishly.

Wolf sat with the boy and gazed into the leaping flames, feeling content. There was a girl on the other side of the fire and after a while Wolf noticed that she and the boy were exchanging glances.

Here we go again, he thought.

Feeling restless, he got up and wandered around the camp, looking half-heartedly for anything of interest.

He saw an older human sitting on the ground at a distance from the fire, chipping at a piece of mammoth tusk with a stone blade. Curious about this rare human who wasn't huddled close to the others after the sun went down, Wolf padded over. The human heard him coming, looked up, and smiled. A pair of amber eyes reflected the leaping firelight.

Wolf froze and his hackles shot up.

The human was a wolf!

You see me, the human said quietly. I hoped you would. I've been waiting for a chance to get acquainted.

Wolf ventured closer, sniffing. The animal was human, no doubt of it, but there was a wolf here too, just under the skin. And other animals and growing things, too, as if this human had more World tucked under their hide than any creature he had ever known.

How can something like you be? Wolf asked.

World is changing, the strange human said. When that happens you can find the places where the skin separating one thing from another gets very thin. With a little practice, you can learn to walk between. Bird. Snake. Fish. I've been them, too.

I've met you before, Wolf said, suddenly remembering. In a dream. I didn't know what you were.

I get around a fair bit in my other pelts, the human said, and smiled. I'm sorry if I frightened you.

Do they know?

The other humans? They do, but they don't really understand. They think I leave this body to visit another one and then return. As long as I bring them back a little useful knowledge, they don't mind too much. It would frighten them to know the wolf came back with me. They're not ready for that truth, if they ever will be. So let's not mention it, all right?

Not a problem. I don't talk to most of them. It just causes trouble.

The wolf-human laughed.

Trouble is what humans excel at, they said. Whenever they find something that isn't any trouble, they get busy making some. Even the oldest, most permanent things will be turning on their heads now that these animals are in World.

Do you come from the Great Mother?

We all do. I've got no special privileges that way. But there is something special about *you*. I saw that right away.

Big sister, Alpha, she told me I was on a path that no wolf had walked before.

She was right.

It's not so bad, being with the humans.

I agree. They're doing well, for now. Did you know they used to survive by scavenging what was left of whatever other animals killed? They weren't hunters to begin with. But they watched the killers kill, and they learned. They imitated the fanged and four-footed, to become more than they had been. They're never satisfied with the way things are. It's their defining trait. When I said World is changing, it's because they're changing it, and so are you.

What do you mean?

One kind of animal *choosing* to throw in its lot with another—there's never been anything like it before, and probably never will be again. The agreement you made to team up with them, that's just the beginning. Together you're making something new, and it's a good thing. The problem with humans is, they don't know when to stop.

I've noticed.

Not being content with things as they are gives them a power over World that they haven't even begun to imagine. But it will take so much from them too. Including wisdom. A time is

coming when they will believe World is only for them, and they will try to eat all of it. They will take it out of the mouths of other animals to stuff themselves sick. They will make more of themselves and fewer and fewer of everything else that breathes and lives in World, and then they will wonder why they are so lonely.

That's horrible. I don't want to be part of it.

It's too late to do anything but go forward, my friend. But I'll tell you a secret, and I hope you'll keep it in your heart.

What secret?

You being here in World, by their side, might just help save them from eating it all.

The next morning the humans got up later than usual and many of them groaned and held their heads, blaming the drink from the night before. That didn't stop them from guzzling more, although now they called the stuff *the hair of the wolf*, which wasn't fair at all, since he'd had nothing to do with it.

The boy and Wolf went exploring in the surrounding hills and Wolf caught a big grey hare. Instead of sharing it as they usually did, the boy carried the hare into the camp, to one of the caves of the new humans. The girl from last night's fire was sitting out front, stitching together a rawhide pouch with a bone needle. She looked up at them briefly, then went back to what she was doing. She wasn't behaving at all like the other girl. Which was maybe a good thing, Wolf considered. That hadn't turned out so well.

Hey, the boy said to the girl.

Hey, the girl said.

So . . . what are you doing?

Bear hunting. What does it look like?

The boy grinned. He took Wolf's kill out of his carrier bag. This is for you, he said. If you want it.

Nice, the girl said, taking the hare from him and examining it. Thanks.

He helped a bit, the boy said, nodding at Wolf, who wasn't sure how his catch had become the boy's to give away. He was going to protest, but then the girl said to him, Come here. He hesitated and then padded over to her. This time he would not make a fool of himself, no matter what.

The girl looked him all over. He glanced at the pouch she was sewing and wondered in alarm if she was considering what she might make from his pelt.

What do you call it? she asked the boy.

It's a he. Our hunters say he's a fire demon.

No, I mean a name. Like yours or mine. Does he have a name?

The boy blinked, his mouth hanging open, then said, I don't know.

You didn't give him one?

Should I have?

Well, he's one of you now, isn't he?

I guess so. Yeah. Yes.

Then he needs a name.

The boy looked at Wolf. Wolf looked at the boy. Each human he'd met had a special word that meant them and them alone. The boy had one. The girl likely had one too. Since he'd left the pack, Wolf had never thought about his. His name was what the other wolves called him, not something he kept for himself. He could have told the boy what it was, but he wanted to see how this was going to play out.

What should I call him, do you think? the boy asked the girl.

You'd better be finished with that pouch, a woman's voice shouted from inside the cave. I need you in here.

Almost done, the girl shouted back.

Well, don't spend all afternoon on it.

The girl rolled her eyes, then looked Wolf over again. She slowly reached out a hand and scratched him softly under the chin. He let her do it.

I shouldn't be the one naming him, the girl said. Think it over for a while. Names are important if you're going to be family. I'm sure you'll come up with something.

Thanks, the boy said. I'd better get going. Guess I'll see you later.

You could come back for dinner, the girl said. If you like. We're having hare stew.

So, the boy said as they walked away. I've got to give you a name. Any thoughts?

Wolf is what my pack called me, Wolf said. He hadn't thought about Alpha and the others for such a long time.

It fits, for sure. But it's kind of . . . obvious.

How did you get your name?

My father gave it to me. It was my grandfather's name. They say I'm him come back.

Come back from where?

The place that people go to when they die. And come back from.

There's a place like that?

Yes. Anyhow, it doesn't solve the problem of what to name you. How about . . . Runner?

That seems kind of reductive. I do other things.

Lightning?

Why lightning?

Well, because you're like lightning.

I'm not.

You are. You're both fast. Get it? Lightning strikes fast—*zap!*—and so do you.

I see. I get it, I think. I don't like it.

Why not?

I don't like lightning. It's usually followed by thunder.

Well, I'm out of ideas.

I'm good with Wolf, really. It's what I am. When you want to call me, just use that.

Wolf, the boy said, trying out the word. All right. It'll have to do. Welcome to the family, Wolf.

Autumn came. The winds stripped the leaves from the trees and snow began to fly.

The humans hunted far and wide. With Wolf along, they were better able to find and stalk prey, and there were great feasts of sizzling meat around the fire. Things were so good the boy's humans decided that instead of trekking back to the lowlands for the season they would stay here in the big camp with the others.

One day the boy gave the girl's mother and father a bundle containing a fresh shank from a deer he'd killed himself, along with a glittering stone he'd fished out of the river. Then the boy built his own cave near that of his mother and father, and he and the girl lived in it by themselves, and Wolf slept just outside the door.

One bitterly cold night the girl said he could sleep inside with them if he wanted to.

He did want to.

Winter was warmer than usual. Rather than disappearing as they usually did in the cold season, the herds stuck around. The humans had a better time of it than even the oldest of them could remember.

Wolf often visited the wolf-human, whom he had taken to calling Many Pelts. You couldn't see the wolf under their human skin, but it was there, alive and warm, and Wolf liked to be near it. Many Pelts lived in a cave of bones they had made for themself at the very edge of camp. When the hunters returned to camp empty-handed, Many Pelts left their body and searched for prey. When they came back, they told the hunters where to

look. When one of the old, frail humans died, Many Pelts sprinkled flowers over the body and sang.

Wolf asked Many Pelts about what the boy had told him, that humans come back after they die.

We all do that, Many Pelts said. Not just humans.

Wolf had always had a vague awareness that he would die, like everything else in World, but spending time with Many Pelts had been putting new and troubling ideas into his head. Lately the thought of his own life's end had more bite.

So when I go to that other place the boy talked about, he asked, I will come back?

It isn't really another place, Many Pelts answered. We're not *in* World, we *are* World. Where else would we go? We feed the earth and then we grow again. Maybe we don't look the same, but it's still us.

I don't understand.

Just know that something always remains from before, from the last time you were here. The most important thing.

Will I . . . remember who I was?

That's hard to say. I think you will, now and then, at odd moments. And then you'll forget again. By the way, I have another secret to share with you, if you're interested.

Sure.

Go up the hill, into the forest. Follow the stream to the place where it begins, among the big, broken rocks. You'll find someone there. Someone you really should meet.

Who?

You'll see.

Wolf followed the stream up into the forest. He could hear the water trickling under its thin shell of ice.

He came to the place where the stream began, just below a slope of huge, splintered boulders.

There was no one here. He sniffed around, wondering if

the wolf-human had made a mistake. In the cold, dead air he caught a living scent. His fur stood on end. He whirled around.

A slender grey wolf was watching him from above, among the rocks. He could tell two things right away: This was a female, and she was alone.

He was too stunned to speak. Then the joy of seeing one of his own kind after so long took over and he bounded toward her.

The female growled a warning.

Wolf drew up short.

It's all right, he said. I'm alone too. I'm happy to see you. You don't have a pack?

They're not here. Where's yours?

They're down below, at the river. But—it's hard to explain. They're not . . .

The female lifted her snout and sniffed.

You smell strange. There's something *not wolf* about you.

There's a good explanation for that. Come, I'll take you to my pack. They'll welcome you, I'm sure of it.

I'll stay here, the female said. There are humans down there.

You've met humans?

Unfortunately.

They're not all bad.

I've got a scar on my flank that says otherwise.

Are you hungry?

Who isn't?

Stay here. I mean, don't go far. I'll bring food.

Wolf ran back down to the camp. One of the friendlier human females was slicing up a skinned boar with a stone knife, getting it ready for the fire.

Wolf squatted down on his haunches near the human. He watched her, his tail wagging, and gave a little whimper.

Go away, fire spirit, the human said. I'm busy.

Wolf whined a little louder and tilted his head to one side. The humans, he'd learned, couldn't resist that move.

Looking for a handout, are you? the human said. As usual.

She tossed a hunk of meat in Wolf's direction. He snapped it up.

You are a menace, the human said, shaking her head. Get out of here.

Wolf dashed back up the hill to the splintered boulders. The female was still there. She watched from the rocks as he lay the bloody meat in the snow.

For you, he said. I can get more.

The she-wolf cautiously came down from the rocks. She snapped up the meat in a few hasty bites, then looked around.

Where did you get that so quickly? she asked.

There's plenty of food down below. Why did you leave your pack?

To find a mate. All the males in my pack are my brothers. How about your pack? Do you have a mate?

I don't.

All sisters?

That's not the reason. Come with me and I'll show you.

I told you, I'm not going down there. But you can stay here with me for a while. If you like.

In the spring the humans noticed a grey wolf hunting alone near the camp.

Some of the young men who had recently become hunters set out with their longteeth to kill it and gain a wolf pelt as a trophy. They hadn't gone far out of camp when Wolf came racing up and planted himself in front of them, growling.

What's wrong with your fire spirit? the hunters asked the boy, who had followed Wolf to see what all the commotion was about.

What is it? the boy asked Wolf, who stood silently with threat in his eyes. Why are you being such a bonehead?

Just then Many Pelts appeared. They stood at Wolf's side.

Go home, Many Pelts said to the young hunters. That one isn't for you.

The hunters backed off and walked away, muttering to themselves, but in the following days the humans kept a watchful eye on the solitary she-wolf. They noticed that when she took down prey, she would carry pieces of it away.

For his part, Wolf spent more and more time gone from camp and the boy. He was also spotted carrying prey in his mouth through the forest.

When Wolf returned in the evenings he would settle in front of the fire without saying anything about where he'd been. The boy noted his reluctance to talk and refrained from asking questions.

One morning Many Pelts found Wolf at the river, where he was watching the boy fish with a barbed stick.

It's time, Many Pelts said to Wolf. Let's take a walk.

Where are you going? the boy asked. I could come along.

It's best if you don't, Many Pelts said.

The boy looked at Wolf. Wolf said nothing.

All right, the boy said. Guess I'll see you later.

Wolf and Many Pelts followed a faint track through the forest. They came to a place where big stones had tumbled down from a cliff face. There were small caves and holes among the fallen stones.

As they approached, the she-wolf appeared at the entrance to one of the caves, hackles up, snarling.

Go away, she barked frantically.

This is a friend, Wolf said. They're one of us.

Many Pelts spoke to the female in a soft language Wolf had never heard before. The she-wolf calmed and settled into an easy slump on the earth in front of the cave. Then she gave a soft *wuff* and out of the cave toddled four small, fuzzy wolf pups.

Wolf approached slowly and sniffed the pups under the she-wolf's watchful eye.

You've done well, brother, Many Pelts said.

The hunting and fishing on the river were very good that spring. There was much rain and the grass was lush. The prey herds grazed close by.

Wolf went back and forth between the camp and the forest, sometimes with Many Pelts but mostly by himself.

One day he finally agreed to let the boy accompany him and Many Pelts to the she-wolf's den. When they got there the cave was silent and abandoned. The she-wolf was gone and she had taken the pups with her. Wolf followed their most recent scent trail into the forest. Then he returned.

They've really left, he said.

They could have joined us, the boy said. Like you did.

She isn't ready to share World with humans, Many Pelts said.

What about you? the boy asked Wolf.

It was just what Wolf had been asking himself. He didn't have an answer. He gazed off in the direction the female had taken the pups.

You've shown them another way, Many Pelts said to Wolf. From now on, the young ones will have the same choice before them that you did. Some will stay in the hills, but a few will follow your lead. Don't worry. They'll return.

It seemed there were more and more humans in World now.

Most of the time they got along fine with one another. They traded, ate and drank together, shared dances and songs. Sometimes they made new humans. Then there were even more of them around.

———

The next summer the girl birthed a pup of her own.

She and the boy let Wolf come close to the new human. He sniffed her inquisitively. She was tiny and hairless and her first wail was tiny too, but ferocious. Her red face was scrunched in on itself like a dried apple.

So this was how a human began, blind and helpless. Like a wolf.

When summer came around again the human pup was walking. Wolf stayed by her, keeping her out of trouble as she toddled around the camp. Whenever he lay down, worn out from chasing her around, she would climb all over him, pulling his ears and whacking him on the snout so that his eyes watered.

It was the best part of his day.

When the pup learned to run, things really got interesting. Wolf noticed he wasn't feeling as lively and tireless as usual. It had been a long winter, longer than most, and maybe he just needed more time to regain his strength. But he had to admit he was having trouble keeping up with this little human.

One sultry afternoon in late summer the pup dozed off on a bison rug outside the family cave and so did he. When he woke up she was gone.

His heart lurched and he sprang up and raced around, frantically sniffing and searching. Finally he caught her scent and followed it out of camp and down a rocky draw to the river.

There she was at the shoreline, picking up little stones and flinging them at the water.

Wolf's heart stopped hammering. She was safe. Nothing bad had happened.

Then he saw the cat.

It was crouched in the tall, dry grass not far from where the pup stood, its limbs taut and ready to spring. A big cat, eyes fixed on its prey. The biggest cat Wolf had ever seen.

There was no time to think. He barked once and burst into a run.

They found Wolf not long after and brought him back to the camp, their shadows hastening before them in the grass.

They set him down on the family bed. The boy was there, and the girl. And their pup, not hurt. Not hurt.

You idiot, the boy said, running a hand softly over Wolf's torn-open muzzle. Water was running from the boy's eyes down his face.

He tried to lick the boy's hand, but his head felt too heavy. All of him felt too heavy, as if he might sink down into the earth.

Then Many Pelts was there. They touched Wolf's side softly with their wolf-human paws.

I'm going now, aren't I, Wolf said. To that other place.

I'm afraid so. That cat really did a number on you, my friend.

And I did one on him, didn't I?

You certainly did.

I hope I come back.

What would World do without you? Many Pelts said. Goodbye, brother, and good journey.

Some time went by. Wolf seemed to have slept and woken again. He could smell a cool night outside. Was the boy still here, with the girl and the pup? He couldn't be sure. His eyes had gotten so weak he could barely make out anything except a silvery glow at the door of the cave. A glow that got brighter and brighter until finally it brushed aside the hanging doorflap and came inside, filling the cave with light.

It was the Great Mother.

It was Alpha.

Hello, little brother, she said.

Hello, big sister. Have you come to take me to the moon?

For a while, until it's time for you to return to World. Are you ready to go?

I think so. I mean, yes, but the boy. The pup. Will I see them again?

No. World will go on, and the humans you knew will return to the grass, and new humans will walk where they walked.

It's hard to leave.

I understand. It will always feel like you didn't have enough time with the humans. You'll want to stay. You'll always want to stay.

Wolf climbed up off the bed, slipping effortlessly out of the agony the cat had left him in, like sloughing off a thick winter's coat. He felt light, and young, and strong.

Alpha led him outside, where all his many brothers and sisters were waiting. They jumped and darted eagerly. They wagged their tails and licked his face.

What would you like to do first, little brother? Alpha asked.

That's easy, he said.

He broke into a run and the pack followed, down the bank and across the river and up into the moonlight.

Afterword

After Boo died I told myself that was it, *no more dogs*. You bring them into your home, you grow to love them, and then they're gone, so soon. Enough loss—we would have to get by without a dog. One evening I was alone in the house and it hit me how much I missed that reassuring presence at my side. I tried arguing myself out of it—the shedding, the barking, the messes—but reason didn't have a chance. We went to a breeder and picked out a puppy. Sam and his siblings were happy accidents—one of the breeding dogs had a forbidden dalliance with the family pet. At the time I was working on a novel that had gotten stalled. Playing with Sam one day, I marvelled at the thought that this carefree goofball was descended from the badass wolves of the ice age. In some ways he was still a wolf.

That thought led to this book. Thank you, Sam.

In my research I discovered that the so-called domestication of wolves probably took place much earlier than was previously thought and was likely more of a mutually beneficial team-up between species. No one knows for sure exactly what happened or how. In gaps like this, a storyteller finds a space to dream.

One thing seems certain: As the wolf became the dog, we became us. Humanity might not even be here at all if we hadn't joined forces with that other clever predator. For the book's opening and closing chapters, I drew on contemporary research and conjecture, including Kay Frydenborg's *A Dog in the Cave: The Wolves Who Made Us Human,* Friederike Range and Sarah Marshall-Pescini's *Wolves and Dogs: Between Myth and Science,* and Pat Shipman's *Our Oldest Companions: The Story of the First Dogs.*

In the end, however, this book is a work of imagination— one I think of, with some misgivings, as a fable. Traditional fables usually feature talking animals who stand in for human virtues and vices, a genre that's fallen out of favour, and with good reason, as we learn more about the remarkable inner lives of other species. The truth is, we turn other animals into people in our stories not because we mistake what they are but because we're not sure what we are, and we've always looked to animals to tell us. If I was writing a dog fable, then, it would be a fable *about* fables, about the many and contradictory tales we've spun about dogs through the ages: what they're for, what they know, how they show us ourselves. Most of all, though, I wanted to celebrate the miracle of these marvellous beings who've been with us on this journey from the beginning and are certain to be with us in whatever future we create together.

"Rescue" riffs on the myth of Cerberus, one of the earliest depictions of a dog in story.

"Escort" is based loosely on ancient Egyptian beliefs about the role of the dog in the soul's final journey.

"Stick" fabulizes the life of Diogenes the Cynic, known as the Dog for his uncouth and sometimes shocking habits. The word *cynic* itself derives from the ancient Greek *kynikos,* meaning "dog-like." How unfair that this wonderful word has gotten attached to such a very undoglike human trait.

"Banana" imagines a sequel to the famous two-line koan that begins the Zen classic *Mumonkan,* or *The Gateless Gate:*

> A monk asked Master Joshu, "Does a dog have Buddha Nature or not?"
> Joshu replied, "*Mu!*" (meaning "no" or "no thing").

"Beast" is set in late medieval France and explores the historical phenomenon of animals prosecuted in a court of law for their "crimes." A jurist named Barthélemy de Chasseneuz (1480–1541) made his name defending animals in such trials.

"Underdog" spins a Klondike gold rush yarn inspired by the ballads of sourdough bard Robert Service.

"Laika" retells the story of the Moscow street dog who was the first living being to orbit the planet. I originally planned to leave her story where history says it ended, then Kurt Caswell's moving, visionary book *Laika's Window* helped me to really see her for the first time, and I needed to give her an afterlife.

"Home" plays a canine variation on *The Odyssey* of Homer, by way of Joyce's Bloomsday.

"Wandering Cloud" is based on a real incident that happened in Colombia in 2017.

Acknowledgements

Thanks and bows to my editor, Anne Collins, and the fine folks at Random House Canada. I am grateful as well to the good people at the Bukowski Agency.

I owe so much to the love and support of my family.

My deepest gratitude to the dogs who have been my teachers.

THOMAS WHARTON has been published in Canada, the U.S., the U.K., France, Italy, Japan, and other countries. His first novel, *Icefields*, won the 1996 Commonwealth Writers' Prize for Best First Book Canada and the Caribbean and was also a 2008 CBC Canada Reads pick. His next book, *Salamander*, was shortlisted for the 2001 Governor General's Literary Award for Fiction and was also a finalist for the Rogers Writers' Trust Fiction Prize the same year. In 2006, Wharton's collection of stories, *The Logogryph*, was shortlisted for the International Dublin Literary Award. His latest novel, *The Book of Rain*, was a finalist for the 2023 Atwood Gibson Writers' Trust Fiction Prize and the 2024 Georges Bugnet Award for Fiction. Wharton currently lives near Edmonton with his family and his best friend Sam.

A NOTE ABOUT THE TYPE

The text of *Wolf, Moon, Dog* has been set in ITC New Baskerville, a cheeky nod to *The Hound of the Baskervilles*. The typeface is based on the serif typeface first designed in 1754 by John Baskerville (1706–75). Baskerville's typeface is classified as transitional, as it was intended to refine the "old-style" typefaces of the period and was part of a larger project to create books of the greatest possible quality. It is characterized by crisp edges, sharp, tapered serifs, high contrast between thick and thin strokes, and consistency in both shape and form.